"You Treated Me Like... Your Mistress."

Jane stared at Adam. "I didn't like it. It's one thing for me to pretend to be involved with you, but I'm not like those other women. I won't be dismissed and ignored when business crops up."

"I don't know any other way to act."

"I wouldn't have done what you did. I don't even know how. How do you do it, Adam? How do you turn off your emotions like that?"

"Believe me, you don't want to know."

"I need something. Because if all that we did before was you scratching an itch…"

"It wasn't," he said at last. "It meant too damned much. You should be grateful the phone rang. I leave nothing but destruction when it comes to personal relationships."

Dear Reader,

Welcome to another passion-filled month at Silhouette Desire—where we guarantee powerful and provocative love stories you are sure to enjoy. We continue our fabulous DYNASTIES: THE DANFORTHS series with Kristi Gold's *Challenged by the Sheikh*—her intensely ardent hero will put your senses on overload. More hot heroes are on the horizon when *USA TODAY* bestselling author Ann Major returns to Silhouette Desire with the dramatic story of *The Bride Tamer*.

Ever wonder what it would be like to be a man's mistress—even just for pretend? Well, the heroine of Katherine Garbera's *Mistress Minded* finds herself just in that predicament when she agrees to help out her sexy-as-sin boss in the next KING OF HEARTS title. Jennifer Greene brings us the second story in THE SCENT OF LAVENDER, her compelling series about the Campbell sisters, with *Wild In the Moonlight*—and this is one hero to go wild for! If it's a heartbreaker you're looking for, look no farther than *Hold Me Tight* by Cait London as she continues her HEARTBREAKERS miniseries with this tale of one sexy male specimen on the loose. And looking for a little *Hot Contact* himself is the hero of Susan Crosby's latest book in her BEHIND CLOSED DOORS series; this sinfully seductive police investigator always gets his woman! Thank goodness.

And thank *you* for coming back to Silhouette Desire every month. Be sure to join us next month for *New York Times* bestselling author Lisa Jackson's *Best-Kept Lies,* the highly anticipated conclusion to her wildly popular series THE McCAFFERTYS.

Keep on reading!

Melissa Jeglinski

Melissa Jeglinski
Senior Editor, Silhouette Desire

Please address questions and book requests to:
Silhouette Reader Service
U.S.: 3010 Walden Ave., P.O. Box 1325, Buffalo, NY 14269
Canadian: P.O. Box 609, Fort Erie, Ont. L2A 5X3

MISTRESS MINDED

KATHERINE GARBERA

Silhouette®

Desire

Published by Silhouette Books

America's Publisher of Contemporary Romance

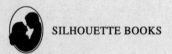

SILHOUETTE BOOKS

ISBN 0-373-76587-8

MISTRESS MINDED

Copyright © 2004 by Katherine Garbera

This edition published by arrangement with Harlequin Books S.A.

® and TM are trademarks of Harlequin Books S.A., used under license.
Trademarks indicated with ® are registered in the United States Patent
and Trademark Office, the Canadian Trade Marks Office and in other
countries.

Visit Silhouette Books at www.eHarlequin.com

Printed in U.S.A.

Books by Katherine Garbera

KATHERINE GARBERA

has had fun working as a production page, lifeguard, secretary and VIP tour guide, but those occupations pale when compared to creating worlds where true love conquers all and wounded hearts are healed. Writing romance novels is the perfect job for her. She's always had a vivid imagination and believes strongly in happily-ever-after. She's married to the man she met in Walt Disney World's Fantasyland. They live in central Florida with their two children. Readers can visit her on the Web at www.katherinegarbera.com.

This book is dedicated to Barbara Padlo
who made me feel like I had family in Chicago
even though I was so far from home.

Acknowledgments:

Thanks to Stephanie Maurer for her editing skills
and insight in the brainstorming stage of this book.
Thanks as always to Eve Gaddy, my critique partner,
who never complains when I send her a chapter and
expect her to read it and send it back the same day!
And thanks to my family who reminds me every day
that happily-ever-after isn't just something I write about.

Prologue

"**P**asquale, you've done well," Didi said as I materialized in front of her desk.

"Babe, call me Ray." No one had lived who'd called me by my given name when I'd been on earth, but Didi was different.

I didn't like the body-disappearing thing, but it beat the alternative, which was me going to hell. I'd been a *capo* with the mob until I was betrayed by one of my lieutenants and killed. My dying prayer for forgiveness had brought me here to Didi—one of God's seraphim, some sort of high angel.

The deal I'd cut was to unite in love as many couples as enemies I'd murdered in hate. I was going to be doing this gig for a long time. *Madon'*, some days it wasn't half-bad, but Didi had a way of getting on my nerves and under my skin.

And when she was giving me a compliment I certainly didn't trust her. She'd sent me to earth in a woman's body one time. Not a hot-looking chick, either, but some old broad.

"There was a reason I was called Il Re on earth," I said to her. *Il re* is Italian for "the king." Yeah, I had the ego and the attitude to carry that off. Didi was always reminding me there was only one king up here, but after successfully uniting three couples, I'd decided to call myself the king of hearts.

"And that reason was…?"

"Don't be smart, babe. You know it's because I'm good at what I do."

"What'd I tell you about calling me babe?"

"Did I call you that? *Madon'*, I'm sorry, Didi. I know you don't like it." I enjoyed giving her a hard time. She looked as if she'd been working in this office too long. Today she was wearing another one of her ugly suits. This one was the color of cooked salmon.

"What's up next?" I asked.

A large pile of colored file folders appeared on her desk next to the jar of Baci chocolates.

"Pick one," she said.

So far I'd pulled from the top and the middle of the pile. I reached for a blue folder about three-quarters of the way down and Didi took it from me. The remaining pile disappeared.

"So where am I going this time?" I asked. What I really wanted to know was if I'd be a man. But asking her that made me feel like a *babbeo*.

She handed me the folder. The location was an island in the Caribbean. Life was looking up. And this couple, Adam Powell and Jayne Montrose, already worked together.

"No problem."

"Don't start thinking about your tan yet, Pasquale. This one is different," Didi said.

Hell, they all were. Didi had yet to give me one assignment that was easy. Matchmaking—Holy Mary!—was hard work.

"How?"

She smiled. My gut tightened. I didn't trust her when she was acting all happy.

"I'll be accompanying you this time."

"*Madon',* is this some sort of punishment?"

"No, babe, it's your reward."

She disappeared before I could respond. Freakin' matchmaker to the lovelorn was one thing. Partnered up with a prissy, bossy angel? Oh, *merda,* this was going to be one hell of an assignment.

One

Adam Powell bit back a curse and tossed his cell phone onto the leather seat next to him. His plane was ready to leave, his guests would be here any moment and Isabella had chosen now to tell him that she wasn't getting what she needed from their relationship.

Frankly, he couldn't *give* her anything else. If diamonds, furs and a brand-new Jaguar weren't good enough, she'd have to look elsewhere.

Normally, being without a mistress wasn't any big deal. He was a grown man; he could live without sex. But the coming two weeks were important to his company. Adam had been trying to acquire La Perla

Negra Resort for the last five years and had been getting no where.

The owner, Ray Angelini, refused to sell his resort to anyone. Out of the blue, Adam had received a call last week inviting him to come to the resort to discuss the possibility of a sale. He had jumped at the chance.

Angelini had asked Adam to bring his wife, which had led to an awkward conversation. Angelini wanted a happily married couple to run the resort, as he and his wife had been doing for the last twenty years.

Adam had always believed in doing anything to close a sale, but pretending to be married was going too far. He told Angelini he'd bring the woman he'd been living with. Angelini had warned him that unless he believed Adam was a man who understood love and relationships there'd be no sale.

"I understand they're both a crock," he muttered.

He left his seat in the back of the jet, exiting the plane. He'd have to make up some excuse for Isabella, and see if Jayne Montrose, his executive assistant, could find another woman who'd meet him in the Caribbean.

Damn, it was hot. New Orleans in the summertime was no one's ideal place to be. The humidity soaked into his skin. He threw his head back, breathing through his teeth. It reminded him of the days when he'd worked the swamp in his uncle's old pirogue, taking tourists for jaunts to see gators and swamp lilies.

God, he'd come a long way from that boy. He intended to go even further, and no woman was going to throw him off track for long.

"Ooo, someone looks pissed," said Jayne, coming up behind him.

He'd hired Jayne because she was sassy and smart. She made life at the office flow smoothly, and in the downtime always made him laugh. "Don't give me any lip, Montrose. Isabella is not going with me and the Angelinis are due in less than fifteen minutes."

"I'm sorry. I told you not to count on her," Jayne said. She reached into the large bag she always carried and drew out a sheaf of papers. "I need your signature on these before I leave for vacation."

"You can't leave on vacation until I find a woman to accompany me to the Caribbean."

"Listen, boss, we've been over this before. I don't procure women for you," Jayne said. She narrowed her eyes and handed him a Mont Blanc pen to sign the documents she'd brought.

Jayne wasn't a particularly tall woman, but she carried herself like an Amazon. Some of the hotel industries' toughest figures backed down when Jayne negotiated with them. Hiring her had been a stroke of genius, and Adam secretly feared someday she'd get tired of working for him and move on.

"I only asked you to get a phone number one time," he said.

That had been a big mistake. Jayne had almost quit

over the matter, and he'd had to do some fancy talking to convince her to stay. Jayne had a strong core of morality and integrity, and she'd do just about anything he asked her to as long as it didn't compromise her own values.

"Once was too many times as far as I'm concerned," she retorted tartly.

Jayne was the best personal assistant he'd ever had. She'd been with him longer than any of her predecessors—almost eight months now.

He studied her as he signed the papers she put before him. Her short cap of brown hair was tucked behind her ears, framing her heart-shaped face. Her eyes were a cool blue, radiating both intelligence and humor most of the time. Her mouth, strictly speaking, was too large for her face. She should have had thin lips, but instead had a lush mouth that made men think of kissing her.

Since Adam had a zero-tolerance policy toward fraternization in the workplace, he tried to avoid looking at her mouth. But he wasn't very successful.

"Why are you staring at me?" Jayne asked.

"I'm not staring at you," he said, signing the last of the papers.

He'd have to cancel the trip and stay home. There were other resorts in the Caribbean. None as elegant as La Perla Negra, but he'd find another property to buy.

"Listen, Jayne, I'm going to have to cancel your

vacation. Without Isabella, Angelini won't talk to me.''

Jayne's eyes narrowed again. "I haven't had more than a day off since I started working for you.''

"You can have time off in a week. I need you here to help me handle this. I'll make it worth your while.''

"How?''

"Name your price,'' Adam said. Early on in life he'd realized everyone had a price. Especially for things they didn't want to do.

She rolled her eyes. "Let's handle it now. Get out your little black book and call another one of your lady friends.''

"I don't have a black book. That's a cliché and women don't like it.''

"You used to have one, right?''

"No,'' he said. He'd never had a black book. He'd never had any problem remembering phone numbers. Strictly speaking, Jayne was right. He could probably make a few calls and find another woman, but he didn't want to. He was tired of the whole thing. And he'd been hoping that Isabella would prove to be different. That perhaps she'd fill that hole that had always been empty inside him.

None of them would be the right fit for this trip to the Caribbean, anyway. Angelini had to be handled carefully, and Adam didn't want to risk anything else going wrong. He needed someone who understood what was at stake. The perfect solution would be for Jayne to go with him.

"Jayne?"

"Yes?" She shoved the papers he'd just returned to her into her bag. Her hair fell forward over one eye and she shifted the tote impatiently to her left hand, tucking her hair behind her ear again.

"Want to come with me and be my mistress?"

A flush spread up her neck. Her mouth opened the slightest bit and for the first time he noticed how creamy her skin was.

She shook her head. "No."

"Why not?" Aside from the phone number incident this was the first time Jayne had said no to him.

"I can't be your mistress—what about Powell International's policy toward fraternization?"

"You wouldn't really be my mistress. We'd act like we were involved. We're not really fraternizing. It would be business."

"That won't work. I don't like to pretend to be something I'm not. I have to take these papers back to the office now, and I booked a nonrefundable airline ticket to Little Rock."

"I'll reimburse your airfare and book you a first-class ticket for the week we return," Adam said.

"I don't know…" She bit her lip and dug in her purse, pulling out a pair of sunglasses and putting them on. "No, Adam, I'm sorry, but I can't postpone my trip to Arkansas."

"Jayne, you're my last hope," Adam pleaded. "I've waited five years to talk to Angelini."

Two hours later, Jayne didn't want to analyze the reasons why she was sitting next to Adam on his jet, bound for the Caribbean. He had said they'd work out the details when they arrived at the resort, which she didn't like. She was a planner. She liked every detail set in stone before she took any action. That way there were no surprises and she could better manage her own experiences.

She'd been determined to say no to Adam's request, but in the end she'd been unable to. So here she was, eating caviar, which she hated, and drinking Moët with the Angelinis. She'd been on Adam's corporate jet twice before, both times to make sure that his every comfort was seen to. In fact, she'd been there this afternoon, arranging for Isabella's luggage to be stowed in the bedroom at the back.

The Angelinis were a very odd couple. Didi was slim and wore a slightly baggy dress in a shade that didn't really flatter her. Ray was short, a little pudgy and balding, but smiled with an effortless charm that immediately put Jayne at ease. They'd invited her and Adam to call them by their first names.

Ray and Didi had flown to New Orleans to see Adam's operation firsthand. Jayne had given them a tour around the city and taken Didi shopping while Adam worked his magic, convincing Ray of all the advantages of joining Powell International. Jayne had a bad feeling that she may have made the biggest mistake of her life in agreeing to come with Adam. She'd been falling in love with her boss since the first week she'd started working for him.

It wasn't his Cajun good looks that drew her, though his thick black, curly hair made her fingers tingle to touch it. Or his wealth, because she'd grown up in a world where money was the only factor in happiness. Or his intelligence, because she'd graduated summa cum laude from Harvard Business School and counted some of the smartest people in the world among her friends.

No, what drew her to Adam Powell was the way he held himself apart from everyone. In her heart she recognized the lonely soul that mirrored her own. But she'd been content to not do anything about it, just secretly dream of her boss and continue working for him.

This trip changed everything. She should have said no. She *would* have said no if any man but Adam had asked her. She'd be on her way to Arkansas right now. She would have accomplished a week's stay in another of the fifty states and be well on her way to achieving her current travel goal to see all of them.

The Angelinis were talking quietly together. Adam put his arm around her, drawing her close to him. He pressed a kiss against the top of her head and she froze. She wasn't going to survive two weeks of this.

Her hand shook and a drop of champagne spilled from her glass.

"Relax," Adam whispered against her temple.

She tried, but she couldn't. He took the champagne flute from her and put it on the table next to his chair.

Then he lifted her hand to his mouth and licked the spilled liquid from her skin. Shivers of white-hot desire spread throughout her body. Adam watched her with those crystal-gray eyes of his.

She saw something there that told her the lust she felt wasn't totally one-sided. Did that mean he had deeper emotions where she was concerned? Was she willing to risk her heart to find out?

She wasn't sure. She'd never been much of a risk taker. She liked to plan and slowly, methodically, move toward her goals.

But she was edging nearer to thirty, and marriage, which had always seemed not important, was becoming more and more a focus for her. She'd tried to make it to the altar once and fallen short. Adam was here now and she knew she might regret it later, but she was going to use the time they had together to explore her fantasies and maybe come out a winner. There wasn't a goal she'd set for herself that she hadn't achieved without planning and hard work.

Decision made, she rested her head on his shoulder. She wasn't sure how to handle Adam. He wasn't like the other men she'd dated. Those relationships had been based on common interests and some really good sex, but none of those relationships had an eighth of the intensity she'd just experienced with Adam's mouth on the back of her hand.

He held her loosely and she closed her eyes, pretending to rest. But closing her eyes was a huge a mistake. She was overwhelmed by Adam. His warm hard body cradled hers. His fingers made idle patterns on her shoulder. And his scent—that spicy, woodsy, masculine scent—surrounded her.

Jayne opened her eyes and stood up. There wasn't an action plan big enough, safe enough, for her to put Adam in it. She wasn't going to be able to do this. Despite the fanciful dreams she'd harbored, she knew that if she and Adam had any kind of personal relationship it would end eventually and she'd be out of a job. Jayne looked around the plane and felt the walls closing in on her. Didi and Ray sat across from her, smiling warmly. Suddenly Jayne stood up.

He raised one eyebrow in question, and she said, "I have to—"

"Change? Yes, you do." Turning to Ray and Didi, he said, "I hope you'll excuse us. Jayne hasn't had a chance to change from her day at the office."

"Of course," Ray said with a smile.

Jayne wondered what exactly she was going to change into. Isabella had about three inches in height on her and at least six inches in bustline. None of her clothes were going to fit.

Adam used his hand on her waist to guide her toward the back of the plane. Once they were inside the bedroom, he let her go and ran a hand through his hair.

"God, this is a mess. I don't think they're buying us as a couple."

"It's not going to help when I come out wearing this outfit."

"Don't worry about the clothing. I had a wardrobe delivered while you ran back to the office to drop off the papers."

She glanced at the bed for the first time and realized it was covered in boxes. She was touched. She knew it was the same thing he did for every one of his mistresses, and it shouldn't matter. But no man had ever bought her clothing before. Adam had an eye for women's bodies and had mentioned to Jayne that nine times out of ten he was right on the mark. He'd guessed her size to prove it.

"You can use Isabella's suitcases for your clothes. I'll leave you to change."

"Adam?"

"Yes?"

"I'll do my best to make this work."

"I know you will, *chère.*"

"*Chère?*" Her heart beat too fast when he called her that in that throaty, masculine way of his.

"It's an endearment."

"I know. Why are you using it on me?"

"We're supposed to be lovers."

She tried not to let it bother her—"supposed" to be lovers. This is a big game of pretend, Jayne, don't forget it, she told herself. "Can I call you stud muffin?"

"If you want me to spank you," he said.

"That's a little kinky, Adam."

He closed the gap between them. Once again she was surrounded by his body heat and his scent. He leaned closer to her and his breath brushed her lips. She grabbed his shoulders for balance as the plane hit an air pocket, jostling them together.

Adam wrapped her in his arms and held her steady until the plane settled down. Jayne was cushioned against his hard chest, and his arms around her were so strong. He held her in a way that promised he'd be able to help her with any burdens she carried. And for a minute she was tempted to let the line between fantasy and reality blur. She leaned her cheek against his chest and listened to the heavy beating of his heart.

"Okay, *chère?*" he asked.

She nodded, unable to speak. He framed her face with his hands and looked deep into her eyes, making her feel as if all her secrets were laid bare before him. She blinked and tried to focus on the present. Fantasy, she reminded herself. This was all one big fantasy.

He cupped her face in his big hands and tilted her head back. She stared up into his dark eyes, every sense on hyperalert. Every feminine instinct screamed for her to reach up and touch him. To bury her hands in his thick black hair and pull his face closer to hers. To bring that mouth of his down to hers and then take the kiss that she'd been craving since the first day she'd walked into his office.

"I never said thanks," he said, his voice a husky growl.

She swallowed and licked her suddenly dry lips. His eyes narrowed and she felt tension move through him. "Are you saying it now?"

He nodded.

"You're welcome," she said.

He lowered his head even more and his breath brushed over her cheek. Oh, God, was he going to kiss her? She shifted to her tiptoes so that only a breath separated them, and she heard Adam groan.

Abruptly he dropped his hands and walked out of the bedroom. Jayne turned toward the boxes of clothing, telling herself that her heart was beating faster because of the charade and not because of the sexual arousal pumping through her veins.

Two

A dam paused outside the doorway. After months of ignoring that made-for-love mouth of hers it was damn near impossible to resist tasting her. And he knew it was only a matter of hours before he gave in and took the kiss he'd been dreaming of since the first day they'd met.

Adam cursed himself for forgetting his own rule. Every time he forgot it he had to relearn painful lessons. Lessons he'd vowed to never forget. And dammit, Jayne Montrose wasn't going to make him compromise.

He'd almost kissed her. And with the bed right there he wouldn't have stopped until he was buried deep inside her curvy little body. That mouth, which had tempted him for so long, had been so close, and only at the last minute had sanity intruded on the moment, forcing him to pull away.

Jayne was his assistant. She took care of everything for him. His office wouldn't function smoothly without her and he wasn't about to let his body screw that up now. He'd already proved time and again that he didn't think well when his hormones were involved.

He wouldn't have believed that Isabella thought they were heading toward something more permanent. But in the end he'd been wrong again. This thing with Jayne was going to have to work because he needed the acquisition of this resort as much to distract himself from the mess his personal life had become as he did to become more successful.

When Adam emerged into the jet cabin the Angelinis were arguing, so he held back until Ray glanced up and gave him a look that seemed to say *women!* Adam agreed.

"Jayne will be out in a moment." Adam returned to his seat, trying to banish from his head the images of Jayne changing.

"Why are you interested in La Perla Negra?" Ray inquired.

Adam's reasons were deeply personal and he wouldn't share them with anyone. Especially not the owner of the resort.

He planned to gut the entire resort area and turn it

into the most commercial tourist destination he could come up with. His reasoning was sound from a financial perspective, but from a personal one it would finally, Adam hoped, lay to rest the demons that had haunted him for a long time. Perla Negra had been the place where his father had fallen in love with his secretary and then left Adam and his mother.

"I'm looking to expand our presence in the Caribbean," he said at last.

"We enjoyed our stay at your Rouge Mansion in the French Quarter."

"I'm pleased. The Rouge was my first hotel."

The door opened behind them and Adam glanced over his shoulder and sucked in his breath. He'd asked Jean-Pierre to send the usual wardrobe over, never thinking of the impact. He told himself it was only because he was used to seeing Jayne in shapeless suits and sedate heels that she looked so damn sexy now.

The floral print dress was slim fitting and cut to a respectable length, but the scooped neckline revealed the ample curves of her breasts. He clenched his hands into fists to keep from reaching for her. This was Jayne, dammit, not some femme fatale.

She cleared her throat and awkwardly crossed her arms over her chest. There was an unexpected vulnerability in her eyes that made him want to stand up and protect her. To vow to always shelter her. A vow he knew better than to make because only fools or weak men made promises to women. And Adam wasn't weak.

She didn't look ready for a vacation, she looked ready for his bed. Her hair was tousled and she'd applied some sort of shiny lip gloss on her mouth. It took all of his control not to go to her and plunder those lips. She didn't need any makeup to enhance that feature.

To prove to himself that she had no impact on him, he deliberately turned away.

"Ah, now you look like you're ready for a vacation," Ray announced.

Jayne dropped into the chair next to him. "I feel ready for one, Ray. I haven't had time to read the file on Perla Negra. I think that means Black Pearl, right?"

What was that fragrance she was wearing? It didn't smell like Chanel or any of the other perfumes he was familiar with. Against his best judgment Adam leaned closer to her, inhaling the scent.

"It does. There's also a legend around the black pearl. Want to hear it?" Ray asked.

"Yes," Jayne said.

Adam closed his eyes and turned away. She was his employee. He wasn't going to act on any feelings he had toward her. He faced the Angelinis, trying to focus on whatever conversation they were having, but it was nearly impossible. Hell, he and Jayne were play-acting. He'd done enough pretending over the years that this should be a walk in the park.

From this angle he could see the curve of Jayne's breast, and when she tilted her head to listen more closely to Didi, he smelled the fragrance of her shampoo.

Didi's eyes lit up as she leaned forward in her seat, as well. "It involves a pirate, a maiden and a fortune lost at sea."

"Sounds like my kind of story," Jayne said.

Adam could scarcely pay attention. For the first time a woman was taking precedence over business. For the first time Jayne wasn't just his girl Friday, but a desirable woman. For the first time a woman was making more than his pulse beat faster, because he realized that Jayne used the same mechanisms he did to hide from real life. The job.

Knowing how important her work was to her, he was determined to make sure their stay didn't become more than a charade. Because he could never keep Jayne on staff if he took her to his bed. It would compromise the standards he'd set in the workplace and the code he'd followed since his father had run off with his secretary years before.

Adam listened to Ray and Didi tell a tale of forbidden love and piracy. He'd read about it already in the resort's literature, which the Angelinis had forwarded to him.

La Perla Negra, a strand of precious black pearls,

had been stolen from a Franciscan abbey by the devious pirate Antonio Mantegna. Along with the pearls, Antonio stole Maria Boviar, the only daughter of a wealthy nobleman. Maria and Antonio were rumored to have been lost at sea.

But the Angelinis at La Perla Negra Resort and Spa claimed that Antonio and his beloved Maria had made their way to the small Caribbean island that was now home to the resort. And that the strand of black pearls Antonio stole was hidden somewhere in the resort.

"Wow, do you offer tours of the resort to try to find the pearls?" Jayne asked.

"We don't have anything formalized, but there *is* a treasure map in every room," Ray explained.

"The real treasure isn't the pearls, Jayne," Didi said.

"What is it then?"

"The treasure is said to be whatever you desire the most."

"Sounds like fun, doesn't it, honeybun?" Jayne put her hand on Adam's arm.

He looked into those pretty blue eyes of hers and saw mischief sparkling in them. Well, at least she hadn't called him stud muffin. He reached out and tucked a strand of hair behind her ear. Her eyes narrowed and she sucked in a breath. She wasn't immune to his touch. A swift rush of triumph swamped him. He knew it would be better for both their sakes if she wasn't aware of him as a man, but he was primitive enough to like it.

"It does, *chère*. We'll have to check it out."

"See that, babe? I told you we'd found the right couple," Ray said.

Adam smiled to himself. He wasn't sure why Ray thought they were the right couple, but it sounded as if he wasn't going to have any problems closing this deal. Unless he counted Jayne and the desire she'd stirred to life inside him.

La Perla Negra rose out of the lush tropical foliage like a queen from a more elegant time. The main building was constructed in California Mission style. Spanish tile roofs gleamed red in the sunlight. Fourteen cottages dotted the landscape around the main resort. The suite they were given had a private balcony overlooking the ocean. One of the other walls was entirely made of glass and looked out over a cove that housed the resort's marina. Jayne slipped off the strappy sandals she wasn't used to wearing and let the thick carpet soothe her tired feet.

As soon as the door closed behind the bellboy, she glanced over at Adam. He'd removed his jacket and loosened his tie. His hair was disheveled from running his fingers through it. This was Adam in work mode. He might look sexy but he'd be all about business, except there wasn't really any work to be done here.

She glanced wistfully at the beach. She wanted to

change out of this dress into something comfortable and go walk on the sand. She'd never been to the Caribbean before. She hadn't planned on international travel until she'd completed her visits to all fifty states.

But this was nice and she vowed to enjoy her time here. Even though she was working she planned to enjoy the island. Could she convince Adam to go with her?

And where was the treasure map? She really wanted to search for it.

The silence once they were alone was charged with awareness. She stared at the man she'd wanted to be close to for so long, and couldn't think of a single thing to say.

"Well, honeybun, what do you think?" she asked.

Adam raised one eyebrow. "That you had better stop calling me that."

"Don't like it?"

"Listen, Miss Sassy, I'm still your boss."

"Are you saying you'll fire me if I call you that again?" she asked him, knowing Adam well enough to be certain he wouldn't.

"Would that make you stop?"

"No," she said.

He threw his head back and laughed. She felt pleased deep inside when she made him laugh. Adam didn't laugh often enough. Most times he was focused so intently on work that he rarely had time for any sort of fun.

Their suite was set up with a sitting area and desk in the main room. She hadn't explored further but there was a doorway that she assumed led to the bedroom. Probably the standard issue double beds were inside. And while she wasn't looking forward to being that close to temptation at night, at least she'd have her own bed.

"What's first on the agenda?"

"I want to make some notes to send back to the office. Did you bring your computer?" he asked.

Clearly, the beach was out of the question right now. And this wasn't a real vacation. "No."

"You can use mine. I have a few ideas. Do you mind if I dictate them to you?"

"No problem, boss. Let me get things set up."

She crossed to his computer bag and started setting up his mobile office, assembling the laptop, printer and fax machine on the large mahogany desk. Adam arranged the chairs and grabbed some snacks from the minibar. It looked as if this was going to take a long time.

"Tell me about yourself, Jayne."

"Tell you what?"

"Something that I can use when we have dinner with the Angelinis tonight."

"Like what?"

"Something only your lover would know," he

said. He sprawled back in his chair, long legs stretched out in front of him.

"Why don't you give me an example?" she asked, balking at the intimate question. Her lovers—and it was barely a plural term—knew little about her. Jayne had learned early on to hide her real thoughts and feelings. Men who said anything about her usually remembered her intelligence and her humor.

"I'm generous," Adam said after a few minutes had passed. Jayne realized she wasn't the only one with barriers. But then, that was one of the first things she'd noticed about him.

"I already knew that."

"How?" he asked, arching one brow in a devilish way.

"I'm usually the facilitator of your generosity."

"Facilitator?"

"That's the résumé spin on having to do your shopping."

He gave her one of those half grins of his that made her forget to breathe. She turned back to the computer and opened a file to distract herself. She labeled it Perla Negra.

"It's your turn."

Something only her lovers would know? She really didn't want Adam to know anything about her that was intimate or personal. She had a feeling that only by keeping a wall firmly between them was she going to survive these weeks together.

"Well, I think that was cheating, but I'll go with it. I like to be outside," she said at last. It wasn't something she'd shared with Ben, whom she'd been engaged to, but Adam was different.

"Why?" he asked.

"I like the feel of the wind in my hair and the sun on my face. We spend so much time in air-conditioned buildings, but I like the heat of New Orleans in the summer. The way it seeps into my skin...I don't know, it makes me feel like I'm really part of the city."

Adam watched her with narrowed eyes and she blinked and looked away. She'd said too much. God, what had she been thinking? "What about you, honeybun?"

"The heat means something to me, too," he said after a moment. "It reminds me of my childhood."

"I don't know much about that time of your life," she said at last. Very little was known about the man. He was a legend in the hotel business because he'd carved his success with his bare hands, buying a run-down old hotel with the money he'd earned drag racing in small towns in the South. He'd turned that hotel into a first-class resort and then used that to launch his international company.

He shrugged and looked away. "I don't like to re-hash the past."

"Then why do you like the heat?" she asked. Okay, she didn't really need to know this, but if she had an action plan to make Adam fall for her, number one would be to figure out what made him tick.

"I didn't say I liked it."

She thought about it for a minute. No, he hadn't. "Why is it important, then?"

"It reminds me of the vow I made when I was fourteen."

"What vow?"

"One secret, *chère*. That was our deal."

"Is that the way your domestic arrangements usually work?"

"Why should you care about that?"

"You started this. If I'm pretending to be your mistress I should know the score."

"You're right. We should discuss the details of our arrangement. You're different than other women I've known."

He was watching her so intently she felt heat spread down her arms and over her body. "Smaller chest?" she suggested.

He gave her one of those vague half smiles. "I don't think so."

Her eyes widened when she realized he was really seeing her. It was as if he were peeling away the layers of clothing and revealing the body she'd always been too shy to put on display. Not too shy, she thought. Too afraid to put on display. She'd never wanted to be like her mother, who used her feminine form to open doors for herself and make life easier.

"How do your lovers treat you?" he asked her at last.

"They treat me like a friend and not an object."

"I haven't objectified you."

"Every item of clothing in that suitcase will."

"You usually dress in frumpy clothes, Jayne. Why?"

"Hey, don't turn this around to me. We're talking about you."

"I like the female form," he said with a shrug.

"I *don't* like mine," she said after long moments had passed.

"Women," he growled.

"What's that mean?" she asked.

"Just that your mouth has been driving me crazy for months and you're worried about how you look in a dress that fits you."

Her mouth. It was an ordinary one, one more plain thing on an average body. "What's so special about my mouth?"

"It's made for kissing," he said.

She swallowed. He leaned forward, closing the gap between them. His breath was minty and she closed her eyes for a minute, remembering that moment on the plane when she'd been surrounded by his body heat. Was he going to kiss her?

Did she want him to? Deliberately she pulled back. She needed to get this back on track, focusing on work. Adam was more complex than she'd dreamed and their time together so far was too…intimate. She had to make a decision. Did she want to become Adam's lover or keep her job?

He became all-business after that, giving her a much needed escape from the intense physical awareness. And in the imaginary box in her head, next to the item that said Adam, she put a big exclamation point and the word *danger*.

Adam congratulated himself for getting things back on a business focus with Jayne. That moment on the plane had been an aberration, and that instant when he'd confessed that her mouth drove him crazy had been simply a brief bit of craziness. He knew how to handle himself around the women he worked with.

Hell, he'd had a hard time keeping his eyes off her mouth. She bit her lower lip when she typed, which he'd never noticed before. Or, at least, never perceived it to be an arousing habit. But having mentioned his obsession with her mouth, he didn't intend to let the subject drop. He wanted to know what she tasted like, and wouldn't be able to rest until he had kissed her.

Jayne followed him into the bedroom and stopped abruptly when she noticed the bed. It was a sumptuous king-size one with a duvet in shades of deep blue. The same color as her eyes.

The rest of the room was done in the same hues. There was an overstuffed chair and ottoman near the window. The sheer curtains stirred in the breeze and a ceiling fan circled lazily.

Immediately, Adam felt the tension he'd brought with him from New Orleans start to dissipate. This was a room that begged the people in it to stop and stay for a while. To cast off worries and relax. Forget about rules and regulations and indulge. Jayne paused beside him and he knew exactly *how* he wanted to indulge.

He'd carry her to that big bed and lay her in the center of it. Then slowly peel away all the layers of clothing covering her luscious body until she was totally bare. Then he'd start with that mouth of hers that he'd been dying forever to taste and explore.

"Well, maybe we should talk about the sleeping arrangements, honeybun," Jayne said.

She sassed him when she was nervous, he realized. She dropped into that shy, quiet mouse mode when he was getting too close to the truth, but when he was scaring her she got mouthy.

But he knew that Jayne wasn't really his mistress, even though she played the part of one. And he was her boss, so he needed to walk a fine line here. Not only for the court of law but with his own conscience, because he'd always believed people who couldn't keep their mind on business shouldn't be in the workplace.

"I'll take the couch," he said gruffly, then was surprised at the scratchy sound of his own voice. Because what he really wanted to do was take her on the couch or any other surface. Damn, he shouldn't be this horny for this woman.

She moved past him into the room. She opened the French doors and stepped out onto the balcony. Adam followed her. A rainstorm was moving over the ocean and a cool breeze blew across his face.

He tipped his head back, imagining that the real world had disappeared and he and Jayne were the only ones who existed.

For a minute, he stood on the threshold studying her. She stared at the horizon and he knew she was searching for answers, just as he was. In his quest to keep business first he'd made a serious miscalculation, one he was going to regret for a long time.

He'd erred on the side of familiarity and factored in the control he took for granted, never considering Jayne outside the office, in this tropical paradise. She called to him just as Eve had beckoned Adam, and he knew that—like his namesake—he was going to follow her on the path of temptation. But he didn't want to lose his Eden.

And Adam had no doubt that his Eden was the world he'd carefully created for himself. The world he'd learned to take for granted because it was intentionally devoid of any of the emotions that made life sticky. Emotions like lust, desire and temptation.

All the things that Jayne called from him without even realizing it. Not things, he thought, emotions.

Those damn feelings he'd never been able to control, despite his experience watching his mother's heart break when his dad had left them. Despite his own experience when he'd been twenty and trusted the wrong woman. Despite all the couples he'd seen cheat on a spouse with a co-worker. He still wanted Jayne.

Damn the consequences, his hormones urged. But his mind knew that a price always had to be paid, and he hadn't decided yet if the price for a few weeks with Jayne was too high.

"Chère?"

She turned toward him and he saw something in her eyes he didn't understand. The wind blew her hair across her face. One silky strand caught on her lips. She reached up to brush it aside and it blew back again.

"We're going to have to share the bed. House-keeping will notice if we don't," she said at last.

He'd thought the same thing. But he knew that if Jayne was in his bed he'd be unable to sleep. Unable to breathe. Unable to do anything but pull her into his arms and kiss that mouth of hers that had been tormenting him for so long.

That strand of hair brushed her face again. This time he caught her hand before she could tuck the lock away. With his free hand, he reached up and swept it back behind her ear, then smoothed his thumb over her lower lip.

"I..."

He tapped his finger against her mouth, stopping the words he wasn't sure she could find. "I've put us in an untenable situation."

"Why untenable?" she asked, tipping her head back.

He leaned a little closer, desperate to taste her. Her breath caressed his face with each exhalation.

Wisdom be damned. "I want you, Jayne."

Her pupils dilated and her breathing speeded up. She watched him with an intensity that made him want to measure up in her eyes. But deep inside, he realized he knew little of what standards she used to measure men.

He doubted he'd be able to meet her needs. Even his mistresses, women he'd chosen because of their materialistic natures, had eventually needed emotions that he'd been unwilling to give them.

Jayne pulled out of his arms. "I'd better go make sure that fax went through."

He should just let her leave. That would be the wise choice, but he couldn't. He didn't know why, but she called to something deep inside him that he'd thought he'd forgotten long ago. "Jayne?"

She pivoted to face him. Her eyes were wide and questioning. Her skin was flushed with arousal and he felt an answering pull in his groin. Yes, his body said, take her now and end all this superficial double-talk.

"Have I misread the signals here?" he asked at last.

She shook her head.

She turned away and he let her go, still unsure that he should let anything develop between them. Not only because of the vulnerability he'd glimpsed in Jayne's eyes, but because of the protectiveness it called from him.

Jayne tugged at the protectiveness he had hidden beneath his armor of cynicism and he wasn't going to let her glimpse it.

Three

"**J**ayne?" Adam's voice was deep and commanding. She fought against the pull he had over her. Forced herself to take another step before she glanced over her shoulder at him.

She wasn't sure what to say to him. It was one thing to imagine having an affair with him, something else entirely to actually do so. In his eyes she saw a deep passion that she'd never really glimpsed in any of the men she'd dated. Just his gaze alone brought her body to readiness. Her pulse beat faster, her breathing came quicker and her center contracted.

If he lifted his hand and crooked his finger, she'd come to him. She'd bare herself to him and take whatever he had to give. She'd stop thinking about all that was wise and sane and just indulge that part of her that had been quiet and lonely for too long.

She bit her lower lip, fighting against her own urges and the potent power in his gaze. She slid one foot forward before realizing what she was doing. She stopped.

Though she always perceived herself as brave and adventurous, she knew deep inside that she was much too practical to ever really do anything that had a high risk potential.

And sleeping with Adam had risk written all over it. Not just on the job front, but on the emotional level. There was a reason she'd felt safe fantasizing about Adam; he was strictly off-limits. She didn't like to examine her own motives in life too closely but knew herself well enough to acknowledge that every relationship she'd ever had had been structured to make her feel safe. And safety came from not risking her emotions.

"What?" she asked at last.

He leaned back against the railing, his shirt pulled tight across his muscular chest. A breeze danced past, blowing a strand of hair across her face and obscuring her view for a moment. She hesitated, then pushed her hair back behind her ear. She'd learned early on that hiding from the things that scared or excited her the most was never a good idea.

"Should I have kept silent?" he asked.

Yes! she wanted to scream. "It would have made the next two weeks easier."

"Not really," he argued. He crossed his arms over his chest and she wished she could mirror his casual pose. But she had neither his experience nor his charm. Her coping mechanisms were smart-ass comments and a quip. And somehow she doubted either one was going to help her through this situation.

What had he said? Something about the next two weeks being hell?

He was right, but she didn't want to admit it. She'd spent a lifetime filling in for everyone. She was an emotional fill-in for her mother, for all the emotion her mom could never coax from her wealthy lovers. For her fiancé, Ben, Jayne had been a substitute for the woman he'd really loved, and when Carrie had returned he'd left her. For Adam, Jayne was a fill-in for his mistress, a temporary scratching of an itch. She was warm and female, but was she willing? The fact of the matter was she wanted nothing more than to crawl into bed with Adam.

For once in her life, she wanted to take what she yearned for, and say to hell with the consequences, the way her mother did. But Jayne had paid the piper one time too many to totally allow herself that freedom.

"Honeybun…" She tried for the light, flippant tone she'd managed so easily before, but it escaped her.

The heart of the matter as far as she was concerned was that she was tired of filling in for others. For once she wanted to have a starring role with Adam.

"Don't get sassy, *chère*. I know you do that when you're nervous. I'm just asking for some honesty here."

She froze. He was the first person to ever call her on that behavior. She crossed her arms over her chest. "You're asking for more than I want to give you."

"Why?" he asked in the silky tone of his that made her want to confess her deepest secrets. He moved toward her with measured steps and she fought the urge to inch backward.

"I need more than you've ever been willing to give your women."

"I'd never group you with any other woman," he said, stopping in front of her. A thrill went through her. He framed her face with his hands, staring down into her eyes. She wondered what he was searching for and if he'd find answers there.

She was touched that he'd said she was in a class by herself. But she knew he'd diverted her question. "I'm serious. I can't enter into a relationship knowing it's not going to last."

"I can't, either," he said, dropping his hands but still remaining close to her.

She knew what he meant. No one started affairs with the intent of ending them. But their own situation was unique. They had two weeks in the Caribbean to enjoy each other. Working together after they'd slept together wasn't something either of them would be able to abide.

"But yours never last," she pointed out.

"You're alone as well."

"Touché." She was alone for a very different reason. She was searching for the missing piece to the puzzle that was her life. And she wasn't willing to try to make the wrong one fit. She had a careful list of traits she was looking for in a man, and she had to be honest. Adam fit the bill on some, but not all of them.

The phone rang before they could continue their conversation. Adam looked as if he was going to ignore the interruption.

"I'll get it," Jayne offered hastily.

"Stay here. We're not finished with this discussion."

Adam left the balcony, and she heard the low rumble of his voice talking on the phone. She hugged her arms around her chest, feeling so much more alone than she'd ever let him know. He was close to offering her something she'd craved for a long time, and she wasn't certain if her plan for life would hold up to a real temptation. It had hurt her when Ben had walked away, but not very deeply because she'd never let him glimpse the real soul beneath the public facade. She'd been unable to hide from Adam from their very first meeting.

Suddenly she couldn't wait any longer for him. She had to get away before she did something really stupid and gave in to the wild impulses flowing through her. There were stairs leading down from the balcony to the beach, and she quickly unfastened the gate and hurried down them.

She wasn't running away…not exactly. She knew she'd have to face Adam, and he'd want an answer to the question left unspoken between them. But she needed to think and plan. Because if she became his mistress she wanted to be prepared for a time when she'd be alone again.

"Jayne?"

She paused near the bottom of the stairs to the beach. The call hadn't been important—not compared to what was happening with Jayne. Just his office informing him they'd received the fax.

"Not now. I need to clear my head before dinner."

"Wait, I'll go with you."

"Why? In case the Angelinis see me?"

He hadn't thought of that, but it was the perfect excuse to go with her. "Yes."

She made a strangled sound and started moving again. Adam hurried to join her. He'd never seen his ultra-efficient assistant like this.

"What's up?"

"Don't be solicitous," she said.

He reached out and grasped her arm. Her skin was

soft and smooth. The full curve of her breast brushed his finger and he realized he'd trade his whole kingdom for an afternoon alone with Jayne. And that was very dangerous.

For a minute everything else in the world dropped away. The sea breeze filled his nostrils and the roar of the surf filled his ears. They were alone in the world, man and woman, and nothing mattered but that.

Her mouth was opened on a sigh and he knew she felt something when he touched her. He leaned toward her, needing that mouth under his. Needing it as he'd needed nothing else since he'd decided that life was better lived alone.

Alone… He pulled back abruptly, dropping his hand. A sheen of tears appeared in Jayne's eyes for a second, then she blinked and wrapped her arms around her waist. He'd been called a ruthless bastard more times than he wanted to admit, but this was the first time he'd really felt like one.

He cursed under his breath and pivoted to face the ocean, staring at the endless water. If he were a different man he'd take Jayne out on a yacht and disappear with her. Forget about the hotel business and promises made when he'd been too young to understand that passion and emotion weren't easily controlled by even the strongest men.

The silence between them felt tense and Adam knew he was to blame, but he didn't know what to say to Jayne. She was so much more vulnerable than he'd have guessed. God, he'd screwed this up royally.

He should apologize but couldn't find the words. "We have to get past this."

"I'm willing to do my job."

"It has to be more than a job or we'll never pull it off."

"It can never be more than a job, Adam. *Never.*"

"Why not? I'm very good at acting the part. The Angelinis will never imagine I'm not the most devoted of lovers."

"I don't want you to pretend to be interested in me. I might forget the ruse and then we'd both be in trouble."

Jayne walked away, and he stood there watching her solitary figure. Instincts he didn't know he had rose in him. He wanted to protect her.

Even from himself?

He ignored the question. It wasn't his intent to hurt her. He just wanted…the same damn thing his father had wanted when he'd come here with Martha all those years ago.

Cursing, Adam deliberately turned away. For the first time he understood a little of what had motivated his father, and he didn't like it.

He'd been toying earlier with asking Jayne to really be his mistress, but he knew now he couldn't. What kind of man took what he wanted at the cost of the innocents in the world? Adam had no doubt that

Jayne was one of the innocents. There had been something in her eyes that had made him feel every inch the cynical bastard he'd known he was from the moment they'd met.

Adam wasn't in their suite when she returned, and Jayne was honest enough to admit she was relieved. She took a shower, dried her hair and then gazed at her face for a minute. She'd made some important decisions on her walk.

Realizing at age twenty-eight that she'd spent most of her life running and hiding wasn't a very comfortable discovery, but it was the truth.

There were two times in her life when she'd wanted to act on her feelings and hadn't. The first had been the one occasion when she'd met her father. She'd been twelve and she'd wanted to ask him if she could call him dad. But she'd hidden in her room and refused to talk to the tall dark stranger who had given her half her genes. He'd never visited her again, and she still felt regret.

The second time had been with Ben, when she'd felt him slipping away from her. She'd wanted to ask him if he had doubts about marrying her, but in the end had kept silent.

This time she'd decided that hiding wasn't an option. She wanted Adam as more than a two-week lover. And she knew the risks involved with the leap she was about to take. During her shower she'd put together a rough plan.

She knew she'd have to start looking for another job right away. Because working together would be… difficult if things didn't pan out.

She put on the plush terry-cloth robe the hotel had provided and applied her makeup with a deft hand. She knew about fashion from her mother, and used all of those tricks now. A little voice deep inside pointed out that she wasn't exactly being herself, but Jayne ignored it. Being herself had gotten her a high-paying job and a lonely town house.

Maybe it was time for a change. She grinned at herself in the mirror, pretending not to notice that her eyes were strained and the makeup made her face seem strange and foreign. She exited the bathroom. Adam was in the process of pulling on his dress shirt. He pivoted toward her as she emerged. She'd thought she was ready to see him again. She'd been wrong.

His chest was bare and muscled. A light dusting of hair covered it, tapering to a thin line that disappeared into his waistband. God, he was gorgeous. Her gaze swept over him time and again and she knew she should look away, but couldn't.

"I didn't realize you were back," she said at last. What an idiot, she thought. Obviously Adam was going to have some doubts about her intelligence if she didn't snap out of this dreamy state.

When he gave her one of his wry half grins, she

realized she always accepted them as signs of real emotion, but perhaps they weren't. "I am. We need to talk before dinner."

That was the last thing she wanted to do. She'd been too chatty earlier. She knew she'd let him see too much of the real woman behind his handy little assistant today, and she didn't want to feel that vulnerable again.

"I don't think so. I just needed some time to adjust to being your pretend mistress."

"That's part of the problem," he said.

She couldn't endure another conversation on the topic, so she crossed to the armoire where the clothing Adam had purchased hung. Jayne usually chose clothes in shades of black, beige or white because they went together. Adam's mistresses apparently didn't worry about that, nor about the amount of luggage they brought with them. There was an entire rainbow of clothing hanging there.

"What's part of the problem, Adam?" she asked, congratulating herself on totally ignoring the fact that he had a scar above his left nipple. Where had he gotten it?

"Pretending. Frankly, you're not very good at it."

"No, I'm not," she said, allowing herself a small smile. "But I think I can handle it now."

"Do you?"

"Yes," she said. Her fingers fell on a boldly colored wraparound skirt and the gold taffeta, sleeveless blouse that went with it. She held both items to her body and glanced at herself in the full-length mirror on the armoire door. Then she took a deep breath, because she was about to take a huge leap and knew from past experience that there would be no one to catch her if she fell. And she'd probably be free-falling for a while.

"What do you think? As good as Isabella?" she asked, pivoting to face him.

He raised one eyebrow. "I can't tell with the robe."

"Didn't she wear one?"

"Yes, but it wasn't made of terry cloth and it never really covered her body."

Oh, man. It figured she'd screw this up. Jayne tipped her chin down and then glanced back at Adam. There was a new tension in his body as he stared at her.

She walked over to the settee and placed her outfit on it. Then she reached for the tie at her waist. It wasn't the smooth move Jayne had intended, for she'd knotted it tightly. Finally the belt was free and dangled at her sides, but the robe stayed closed.

She didn't know if she could do it. In fact, she couldn't. She must have island fever or something to have thought she could—

"Chère?"

She felt like a little mouse the moment before a big eagle swooped in for the kill. But steeling herself, she tipped her head to the side and gave Adam a once-over that left no inch of him unexplored. "Honeybun, you look good."

She'd expected him to throw his head back and laugh, but instead he took a few steps toward her, then reached out and touched her face with gentle fingers. She longed to touch him as well, but despite her new resolve, she had a lifetime of scruples keeping her hand firmly by her side.

"I don't think I've ever seen you wear makeup," he said softly.

He brushed his thumb across her cheek, starting a chain reaction deep inside her. Sensation spread down her neck, across her chest, making her breasts feel heavy and full. It continued downward, pooling in the center of her body. She closed her eyes briefly, which made each stroke of his thumb feel more intense.

Then he slid his hands down her neck and pried her fingers from their death grip on the lapels of her robe. He held both of her hands in one of his while using his free hand to cup her jaw and tilt her head up toward him.

In his eyes, she saw a million messages, but couldn't decipher even one of them. He leaned in close and brushed his lips over hers. She shut her eyes once more and quieted the inner voice that said she was in deep water and there was no sign of a life-guard. Instead she indulged in kissing the man who'd made a place for himself inside her quiet soul.

Four

Passion had always been the one area where Adam considered himself an expert, but Jayne made him feel as green as a boy with his first woman. Instead of smooth and practiced, he was grasping and hungry, thrusting his tongue past the barrier of her teeth and taking her mouth the way he longed to take her body. Deeply, thoroughly, leaving no space unexplored.

He slid his hand down her neck to the opening of her robe. Freeing her wrists, he held her loosely, grasping her lapels and slipping his forefinger under the terry cloth. Stroking gently, he moved it closer and closer to her breast.

She moaned deep in her throat, and something savage was unleashed inside him. It felt as if he'd never been with a woman. All the finesse he'd carefully cultivated over the years to protect himself from this kind of emotion was gone—stripped bare so that nothing was left but the rough-edged man who'd grown up in the swamp. The man who'd had to leave that life behind for vengeance.

He didn't want to dwell on that. Not now, when he finally had Jayne's made-for-sin mouth under his. She tasted just as he'd expected her to taste.

Headily, he drank from her lips, pulling back only when he became aware of the low sounds coming from her throat. He lifted his head to glance down at her. Her eyes were heavy and her mouth—damn, her mouth was wet and lush. Her lips were redder than usual and he couldn't help it, he had to see if her nipples had also darkened.

He pulled the sides of her robe away and stared down at her body. She was wearing a pale green bra of lace and silk, which hardly contained her straining breasts. Each breath she took thrust them into stark relief—miles of creamy skin framed by the light colored robe.

His erection, hard before, strained even more. He skimmed his gaze down her body, over the small swell of her belly to the matching mint-green panties covering her. He swallowed and reached out, caressing her from neck to navel.

"Do I look like your mistress now?" she asked.

He didn't want to talk. Didn't want any reminders that this was Jayne standing in front of him and not some woman he'd made arrangements to have in his life for three months.

But because it was Jayne and not some other woman, talking in the middle of this seemed right somehow. "Not yet."

"Not yet?" She took a half step back from him and slid the robe down her arms, holding it there, and angling her hips to one side to pose like a centerfold. "How about now?"

"Jesus, woman," he said, and closed the gap between them. He freed the front clasp of her bra, peeling back the cups to expose her breasts. Her nipples were the same color as her lips, and hardened under his gaze.

"Now?" she asked huskily. But there was little of the vamp that had been present just moments earlier. In her place was the shy Jayne he always sensed beneath the surface.

He took her hands from the sides of her robe. "Not yet."

He rubbed the rough terry cloth over her nipples until she bit her lip to keep from crying out, and then lowered his mouth to once again kiss her. Kissing Jayne was an addiction he doubted he'd ever recover from. Only when her hips began lifting toward his did he break the kiss and step back.

"Now," he said.

She stood there in front of him, her robe open and her bra pushed out of the way. She should have looked vulnerable in that moment, but Adam knew the person with the real weakness was himself. He stared at her. A lifetime of scruples meant nothing when he was faced with the very real temptation of this woman.

He struggled against the emotions running rampantly through him, and settled on the one thing that had never let him down: lust.

He pulled her to him again. This time when he lowered his head, he thrust his tongue deep into her mouth. She met each thrust of his tongue with one of her own. God, she tasted sweet.

Her hips rocked against his and he nestled his hard-on into the notch of her thighs. She was so hot he could feel her through the layers of her panties and his dress trousers.

She rocked against him and he slipped his hands down her back, tracing her spine and then clasping her hips. Holding her still so he could rub his cock against her. He groaned and threw his head back. She felt incredible, just as he'd known she would.

"Adam?"

"*Oui, chère.* That's it," he said, moving against her, feeling her body pick up a rhythm that had only one surcease—in climax. He rubbed his chest against her breasts. Her nipples stimulated him and he gritted his teeth to keep from coming in his pants.

She called his name again and he traced the curve where her legs met, finding her humid warmth and teasing that opening before slipping one finger under her panties and touching her. He thrust into her body and felt her tighten around his finger. He added a second and placed his thumb over her pleasure bud, until he felt her clenching around his fingers.

He lowered his head and swallowed the sounds she made as she came, then cradled her against his chest and tried to ignore the throbbing in his groin. Adam knew there was no justifying what had happened here. They'd taken a step that couldn't be undone.

Jayne clung to Adam dizzily. Her body still throbbed from the sensations he'd evoked in her. A sheen of sweat coated her skin, and as satisfying as her climax was, she ached to have him take her. Ached to have him possess her, and maybe, in some small way, possess him as well.

She didn't know what to say. With the men in her past she'd been in control of herself. Adam had sent her carefully ordered world topsy-turvy and she was floundering. She didn't like it.

He tipped her head back, gazing down at her with those gray eyes of his. She searched for some kind of emotion there and found tenderness. He stroked one finger down the side of her face, then cupped her jaw gently, rubbing his thumb over her bottom lip.

She'd never felt so cherished by a man—by any

man in her entire life—as she did by Adam at that moment. He bent and lifted her in his arms, carrying her toward the king-size bed.

"Chère—"

His PalmPilot beeped. For a moment Jayne didn't know what it was. A meeting reminder. She'd scheduled a conference call for Adam with his vice-president, Sam Johnson. Let it go, she thought. And in her mind this became a sort of test. She schooled her expression to reveal no emotion as he set her on her feet. He left her side, glanced at his PalmPilot, and picked up the phone, his gaze never leaving hers and still filled with that tenderness she didn't really understand.

Then he glanced away and reached for his notepad. He turned from her and sank down on the bed, jotting notes and speaking into the phone in that rapid-fire way that meant he was angry. She knew in an instant that he was scarcely aware of her presence anymore.

She'd been dismissed. Finally she felt like a mistress, and it wasn't a feeling she particularly liked.

She felt used and cheap. She felt…aching and angry, and only her own self-control allowed her to turn away from him at that moment when she wanted instead to confront him.

She took the clothing she'd removed from the wardrobe and entered the bathroom. The woman she saw in the mirror was one she didn't recognize.

Her lips were full and flushed from his kisses. Her

hair fell around her face in disarray. Her nipples were still hard and her skin was exquisitely sensitive.

She ignored the urge to go back into the bedroom and rail at Adam. Instead, she calmly refastened her bra and dropped the robe to the floor. She donned her skirt, which ended at midcalf, and then put on the blouse. Other than being cut a little lower in front it was almost something she'd wear.

She fixed her hair, touched up her lipstick and hung up her robe before leaving the bathroom. Adam was still on the phone when she emerged. He didn't glance up from the notes he was making, and Jayne told herself it was nothing personal. Nothing that a pretend mistress should get angry about, but it didn't change the fact that she was riled up.

She found the shoes that matched her outfit and stalked out of the bedroom. She didn't know what to do now. Was she supposed to sit around and wait for him? Her mom would know, but Jayne wasn't calling her mom.

Instead, she explored the room in hopes of finding the treasure map.

There was a laminated notecard with typed instructions. She read the note, went to the reproduction print hanging on the wall and pulled on the frame carefully. It swung out from the left side and the map was in the pocket on the back of the frame. She read the legend again. And though Didi had done a nice job with the storytelling, the one on the map was more elaborate. Something out of a pirate romance novel.

The promise of finding your heart's desire was quixotic. How many people *really* knew their hearts and themselves well enough to find what they desired more than anything else? Jayne knew that if she were honest with herself she desired two things at this moment—Adam's head on a platter and a repeat of what had just happened, but with a different conclusion.

She couldn't stop the wild race of emotions through her body and she bounced between sexual frustration and a deep feeling of rage that she didn't know how to restrain.

The light on the extension blinked out and she knew he was off the phone. She waited for him to come to her, but he didn't. She heard the rush of water in the bathroom and realized he was getting ready for dinner.

She put the map down and entered the bedroom, skimming his notes. They were neatly written and had several instructions on them for her. Either what had happened between them was so commonplace in his world that it had no effect on him, or he had better mastery of his emotions than she did.

She hoped for the latter, but life had taught her that just because she wanted something to be true didn't always mean it would be.

"Good, you found my notes. I need you to send a few e-mails. I think we have time before we have to meet the Angelinis for dinner for you to do that."

He had buttoned his shirt and turned away from her to tuck it in. She felt as if she'd just dreamed the sensual encounter they'd had less than thirty minutes ago. He was acting the way he always acted around her.

Let it go, Jayne, she told herself. But she couldn't. She'd put something on the line here and she'd thought, maybe foolishly, that Adam was doing the same. Why the hell wasn't he as deeply affected by that embrace as she had been? Had he seen that damn flaw of hers that every man in her life had found? Why couldn't she fix it so she never had to feel this way again?

"*Chère,* you okay?"

"Don't."

She picked up the notepad and crossed the room, escaping to the living room. She'd send his damn e-mails and gather her wits. She needed to confront him about this, but not now when her blood felt close to boiling and her temper was about to get the best of her.

As she brushed past him, the scent of his aftershave wrapped around her like a lover. Making Adam fall in lust with her was incredibly easy. Making him fall in love with her was a different matter altogether.

* * *

Adam watched Jayne leave their bedroom and clenched his fists. Dammit. He looked for something to kick but didn't want her to see how deeply she'd affected him.

He thrust his fingers through his hair and stood there for a moment. He'd hurt her. God, if she looked at him with those wounded eyes one more time, he'd forget the good sense that the beeping PDA had brought back, and take her to bed.

He'd love her six ways from Sunday and not let her leave the room for the rest of their time here. To hell with business deals.

But his meeting had interrupted him before he'd gone too far. That kiss—hell, he needed another one—was going to be an aberration. He'd decided earlier against asking her to be his mistress in truth. And nothing had happened to change his mind.

He straightened, quickly knotted his tie, shrugged into his dinner jacket and smoothed down his hair. He'd put on too much aftershave, trying to drown out the scent of Jayne, which had permeated the bathroom. He'd been unable to resist burying his face in the robe she'd worn. Her scent was nearly irresistible to him.

He paused in the doorway. Jayne sat at the table where they'd worked earlier. She was typing at the computer, but her ire was clear in every movement she made. The outfit he'd ordered for her looked incredible. Though he knew it was hard on his libido, he was glad to see her dressed in clothing that fit and enhanced her feminine form.

"Almost done?" he asked.

"Sure thing, honeybun."

All of the teasing was gone from her voice, and he knew that if he took her down to dinner with the Angelinis now, they'd know something was wrong.

"You work too hard," he said, keeping his tone light. He walked over to her and put his hands on her shoulders, massaging them. But the feel of her soon had a pronounced affect on his body. He hardened and had to close his eyes for a minute, tipping his head back to reclaim his control.

"You're my boss," she said.

He removed his hands and sank down in the chair next to her. She finished typing the e-mail and then sent it. He noticed she'd checked off several items on the notepad and put the in-process symbol next to a few more. Some of the items had names written next to them and he realized in the time it had taken him to change she'd delegated his entire list of to-do items.

She shut down the computer and turned to face him. "How do you do it?"

"Do what?" he asked. He wondered how she'd accomplished so much so quickly. But he shouldn't be surprised. Jayne was the only assistant he'd ever had who kept pace with him in the office.

"Turn off your emotions. I can't do that."

"I don't."

"You do. I'm still…never mind. I'm mad at you."

"I know," he said. He had a feeling she was still frustrated sexually, as well. That one brief climax wasn't enough to have satisfied the passion that ruled her under that calm surface. And he'd never meant to stop before they'd made it to the bed and he'd taken possession of her.

"You treated me like…your mistress. I didn't appreciate it."

Adam struggled against what she was saying. Jayne was unique because for so long he'd felt safe with her. Her humor had made it impossible for him to keep his usual distance, and now he wished he had.

"I…"

"I don't like it, Adam. It's one thing for me to pretend to be involved with you, but I'm not cut out to be like one of your women. I won't be dismissed and ignored when business crops up."

He thrust his hand in his hair again and then realized what he was doing. He reached instead for Jayne, but she flinched when he touched her this time. Protecting himself was coming at too high a cost. And he didn't want Jayne to have to pay it.

He wanted to fight dragons for her. He wanted to protect her. To be her damn white knight. Where the hell had that come from?

He didn't know. But he knew that the feeling was the truest emotion he'd felt in a long time. And he knew that he couldn't tell Jayne. He'd feel even more foolish—no, vulnerable.

"I don't know any other way to act," he said.

"What, women only fall into two categories—lover or co-worker?"

"Yes. And don't say it with such disdain. I don't notice a man hanging around in your life."

"I date."

"Yes, but you never involve them in your life. They fit neatly into a category, as well."

"I wouldn't have done what you did. I don't even know how. How do you do it, Adam? How do you turn off your body like that?"

He couldn't. Didn't she realize it was all an act? One he'd fought hard to master a long time ago, when he'd realized that he wasn't immune to the weaknesses his father had. When he'd learned that women wielded a power far greater than any female ever realized. Especially Jayne who was a temptress worthy of her own legend. She had the ability to make him lose control. To lose his focus on work.

"Practice," he said. He glanced down at his watch and noted they didn't have a lot of time before dinner. He stood, and Jayne rose as well.

"What kind of practice?"

"Believe me, you don't want to know."

"I need to. I need some explanation. Because if all that before was you scratching an itch…"

He said nothing, just watched the emotions roll

across her face, realizing Jayne had no shield. And he didn't want to teach her to use one.

"It wasn't," he said. "It meant too damn much, which is why you should be grateful to Sam. I leave nothing but destruction in my path when it comes to personal relationships," he told her, and walked out of the room.

Five

"**A**dam?"

He paused but didn't turn around. It should have made words easier to find, but didn't. She hurried after him and took his arm in her grasp, making him face her. His muscles clenched under her fingers and she wished she'd taken more time earlier to explore his body.

"What?"

"You can't just walk away after saying a thing like that."

"I have to. Don't get your hopes up, *chère.*"

"What hopes?"

"That what we have here can mean anything once we return to the real world."

The softest look came across his face and he cupped her jaw with a gentle hand. Tilting her head, he dropped a kiss on her lips. It was feather soft and it confused her. Adam was telling her something with this embrace. But she didn't understand.

It felt like goodbye. Then he dropped his hand and moved past her on the path. She touched her own lips, watching him leave.

A rush of joy flooded her and she knew it was foolish to let his comments mean that much to her. But they did. She steeled her heart and warned herself that the sight of him walking away from her was one she should get used to. But she didn't feel angry anymore.

Instead, she was conflicted with emotions about the complicated man who was so much more than a boss. His words made her ache for the boy he must have been. She'd felt many things for the complex man she was half in love with, but sympathy wasn't one of them until now.

She'd suspected there were dark secrets from his childhood that drove him to be so successful. He spoke little of his parents, and Jayne had imagined he'd had an upbringing like hers. She'd never suspected that he'd experienced the other side of the coin. Because in her heart she suspected his father must have left Adam and his mom for a woman like her mother.

Jayne ached deep inside in the emotional place that

reminded her she wasn't as mature as she wanted to be. The place that made her remember what it felt like to watch her father through a slated-wood closet door. That place that was still recovering from Ben's departure and didn't want to ache again.

She locked the door to the suite and headed toward the main hotel building, where the bar and one of the restaurants was housed. She had to get her focus back on work. It would be nearly impossible to ignore Adam, but that was the only way she was going to be able to survive these two weeks in the Caribbean.

The cobblestone path was lined with verdant bushes that smelled like the inside of a florist shop. She stopped by a hibiscus and plucked a bright red blossom, tucking it behind her ear. She was tired of being one bloom that never opened to the sun. Tired of living her life on the sidelines. Tired of not taking the biggest risk life had to offer.

Mentally she started a to-do list for when she returned to New Orleans. She'd have to find another job and prepare Adam to have a new assistant.

She finally reached the building and crossed the lobby. Standing in the shadows, she observed Adam, who sat alone at the bar. There was a tension in him that she hadn't noticed since the first few days she'd started working for him. She knew he was in a bad space, and that she was partially responsible for that. Ben had told her one time that just looking into her

eyes made him feel guilty. She didn't really understand what he'd meant by that.

But for some reason, her code of morality shone
around her, and many people had a difficult time lying
to her. She also knew that she'd made things as difficult as possible between herself and Adam earlier.
She'd wanted him to feel a little of the pain and in-
decision that was swamping her.

It looked as if she'd succeeded. He tilted back his
head and drained his whiskey glass in one swallow.
She knew he was drinking single malt. It was his
favorite.

She knew so many superficial things about him that
she'd been able to convince herself she loved him.
But only now did she realize how much she still had
to learn.

"How do you like my island, *amica?*"

Jayne turned to face Ray Angelini. He wore a well-
tailored suit and held a cigar loosely in one hand. He
appeared much more at ease here than he had on the
plane.

His island was turning into her own personal prov-
ing grounds, Jayne realized. She had to face herself
and make some tough decisions.

"It's very nice. Adam has already started making
notes on the resort. He's so excited that you're talking
to him about selling it."

"I know he is, but I don't want your business opinion. How do you like the romance of the island? Didi

thinks some couples need to be pushed along, but I think each relationship has its own timetable.''

Jayne felt as if she was under a spotlight. She knew that if she said the wrong thing she might ruin this deal for Adam. And Perla Negra was important to him. ''Adam and I have found that. We worked together for a while before we started our relationship.''

''I can see you two are very close. Let's go join your man.''

Adam wasn't *her* man. Not really, but that didn't stop her pulse from racing as they approached him. Everything solidified in her mind and she wished he would be her man. Nothing would thrill her more. Love was the grand adventure she'd been searching for for a long time. And Adam was just the man to give it to her.

Adam watched Jayne like a man with an addiction. He took another swallow of his wine and knew he'd had too much to drink. He'd had three glasses of whiskey before she'd joined him.

And once they'd sat down at dinner he'd continued to drink more than eat. God, she was lovely tonight. She had a red flower tucked behind her ear, and she seemed to glow from within. He wasn't sure where that had come from because when he'd left her she'd seemed shattered and angry.

He felt the weight of that on his shoulders and reached again for his wineglass before realizing that getting drunk wasn't the solution. He picked up his water glass instead and drained it, signaling the waiter for a refill.

Ray had ordered for them all and they were dining on some of the best seafood Adam had ever tasted. And he'd grown up on the Gulf, so it was hard to impress him. But the resort's chef was first-class and the food was impeccable.

For all that, Adam barely tasted it. His concentration was solely on Jayne. Something had changed in her tonight and he wasn't going to rest until he'd figured out exactly what.

"I looked at the treasure map this afternoon. It's pretty easy to follow," she told him when silence fell between them.

Jayne had kept the conversation going all evening. Adam wondered bitterly if he should give her some sort of bonus. He felt as if she was showing him what he'd be losing if he didn't stop trying to seduce her. And his guts felt raw and exposed by the lesson.

She's just a woman, he reminded himself. There's an entire sea of them out there. But his soul rebelled. There wasn't another person in the world like Jayne, and something deep inside him knew it.

"There are a few surprises along the way, but for the most part, we want our guests to find it," Didi said.

There had been a little tension between Didi and Ray at the beginning of the meal, but Jayne had managed to put them both at ease. She had real talent for making everyone comfortable and happy.

Except him. The brighter she shone at the dinner table, the worse Adam felt. He knew he'd acted like a bastard earlier and he knew that a better man would have apologized. But he wasn't going to.

"So, *compare,* what is it you want more than anything else?" Ray asked him.

Jayne, he thought. But instead he smiled like the salesperson he'd been when he first started out in this business. "Perla Negra."

Ray laughed. "Nice. Truly, what is it you desire most? We had a couple here last month who wanted nothing but wealth."

That pissed him off. People always wished for money, as if it was the answer to the world's problems. But the truth Adam had learned as a young man was that unless you worked for the money it was empty, and left a man feeling like a hollow shell.

"Adam?"

He shook his head to clear it and reached again for his water glass. "I'm already a wealthy man. I don't need a 'treasure' to bring me what I want. I know how to go out and work for it."

He felt Jayne's hand on his thigh under the table— a small warning pinch—and then she started to pull away. He clasped her hand in his and held it in place. It was the first time she'd even acknowledged he was at the table. Despite the way she'd sparkled, she'd left him alone in the shadows.

"Allowing that, then Perla Negra will be yours by effort and not treasure hunting. What's the one thing you want but can't have?" Didi asked.

Adam rubbed Jayne's hand against his thigh and glanced over at her. She stared up at him, her wide blue eyes, darker than midnight, watching him with a kind of expectation that made his heart beat faster. "I want Jayne."

Her sexy mouth parted and her pink tongue darted out to wet her lips. She tilted her head to the side and said nothing, but he could see her pulse wildly beating at the base of her neck. Unable to resist, he touched that pulse with his free hand. Caressed the spot where her life pounded through her body.

Her skin was soft, and gooseflesh spread out from his fingertips, letting him know she was exquisitely sensitive. He made a decision he wasn't aware he'd been mulling over: he was going to have Jayne as his mistress.

"Presumably she's already yours," Ray said.

The spell was broken and Adam turned his gaze to their other dinner companions. "She's the only unpredictable thing in my life."

Ray nodded and Didi pursed her lips. "What about you, Jayne? What do you want?"

She shrugged. And Adam realized that while she seemed to be frank and up-front, letting the world see her as she was, there were a lot of layers to this woman. "I'm not wealthy like you are, honeybun. So money would be nice. That way I could sleep in every morning and get up when I wanted to, but…"

He turned away from Didi and Ray, looking down at Jayne, watching her as she bit her lip and closed her eyes for a second. When she opened them he wasn't sure whether she was going to tell them what she really wanted, or what she thought they would like to hear.

"I've always wanted a real family."

"Kids?" Adam asked.

She nodded. "I want the whole shebang. Kids, husband, in-laws. I want to be part of a big family."

"I'm an only child," Adam said.

Her smile turned so sad that for a minute he felt as if he'd been punched in the gut. But that didn't make sense. Jayne was his assistant, and if he played his cards right, maybe his mistress. Why should he ache because he knew he could never give her the one thing she craved?

"Then you better get busy with the babies," Ray said.

Didi punched him in the arm and gave him a warning look. "Babe…"

"Never mind. We have a jazz band playing in the lounge later. Will you two join us for dancing?"

"Not tonight. I promised Jayne a walk on the

beach. She likes to be outdoors, since we spend so much time in the office usually.''

Didi nodded and Ray looked pleased with himself. Jayne's hand turned under his and he wrapped his fingers around hers and held them with a desperation he wasn't sure he liked.

The night breeze was warm and steady as they walked down the tiki-lit path toward the beach. ''It probably would have made more sense to go with the Angelinis to the bar. You could have made more notes.''

''I know what I'm doing, *chère*. I've been running the company for a long time.''

''Sorry. I guess I'm too used to being your assistant. And Ray and Didi both seemed to be buying us as a couple. I was worried about that for a while.''

''I wasn't.''

''Why not? How could you be so confident?''

''You've never let me down.''

She wanted to smile but knew he was being evasive again. ''You go from being this dream man to being a cold robot quicker than I can snap my fingers.''

''I'm not cold, not around you.''

''But I am,'' she said.

He didn't respond to that. Jayne felt a little of her determination waver. They arrived at the beach. ''Still want to go for a walk?''

''Do you?''

"Yes."

Adam sat on a bench to remove his shoes and socks and roll up the bottom of his pants. She slid off her sandals and set them next to his on the bench. The sand under her bare feet felt wonderful, grainy and textured and a little cold.

Then Adam grasped her hand loosely and they started walking down the beach. The only sounds were the roar of the surf and the call of a night bird. It was a Hollywood moment—a couple under a full moon walking along the surf. But in her head Jayne realized that nothing was picture-perfect. Not her, not Adam and not the dreams she'd had as a girl alone in her room.

There was a reason why she had a million to-do lists in her life. And that reason was she had to be in control of everything. Too much of her childhood had been unpredictable.

"Do I really leave you cold?" Adam asked.

"Sometimes. I guess that wasn't very fair. But I'm not feeling myself."

He tilted his head and looked up at the stars. "I can't give you more."

"Why not? Powell's fraternization policy?"

"Partly."

She waited.

"I've seen lives destroyed because of lack of control, *chère*. And I don't want that to happen to you."

"That's the second time you've mentioned destruction. But you don't destroy anything. In fact, you build some of the most luxurious resorts in the world."

He stopped, dropping her hand and facing the ocean. "I'm careful in my personal life. You know that. I pick women who don't…"

"Want more than you give them?"

"Yes."

"Why? I can't imagine you grew up thinking you'd just have a string of mistresses—they're easier than wives."

"But I did."

Suddenly she felt chilled and stepped a little closer to Adam. He sensed her shiver and slipped his dinner jacket off, draping over her shoulders. Then he wrapped his arm around her and pulled her close to his side.

"Why would you choose that? It's such a cold life."

"You sound like you know something about it."

She shrugged. She wasn't going to tell him her feelings on mistresses.

He tugged her into his arms. "This is a night for romance and I don't want to waste it talking."

He lowered his head, but she pulled back. "I'm not going to be blinded by sex."

"Blinded by sex," Adam said with a chuckle. "Jesus, Jayne, you kill me."

She smiled to herself. But she wanted some answers. "You were trying to distract me. Why?"

"I'm not sure," he said. He slipped his hand into hers again and tugged her toward the water. "Let's play."

"Okay, but I still want to know more about your relationships."

"That's not a very nice topic to bring up with a new lover."

"But we're not really lovers."

"I think we will be."

"Me, too," she said softly.

The waves ran over their feet, cool but not too cold, and they stood there staring at each other. Finally, Adam leaned down and brushed his lips against her cheek. "I saw what cheating and infidelity can do to a family. I vowed to never put anyone in that position."

"You're so strong. I don't think you'd ever do that."

"I'm my father's son, Jayne. We haven't been out of New Orleans an entire day and already I'm contemplating breaking one of the company's rules and my own vow to never get involved with a woman who works for me."

He removed his hands from her body and stepped back. She watched him for a long moment and realized that shadows of the past were once again reaching out to darken the future. She'd felt it every day of her life, but never thought about Adam that way. Until now.

"I think you're better than that."

"Sure you do."

"I do."

"Prove it," he said.

"How?"

"Kiss me and make me believe it."

"Okay," she said. Leaning up on tiptoe, she pulled his head down to hers and whispered his name against his lips. "Honeybun, prepare to be wowed."

Six

Jayne's mouth seduced him with light brushes of her lips and then tentative touches of her tongue. A shudder ripped through him. God, he needed her with a desperation that compared to nothing else he'd ever experienced.

He hardened in a rush and slipped his hands under his jacket, which was draped over her curvy body. He ran his palms up and down her back, cupping the lush shape of her hips and pulling her closer.

The game that he'd started back at the airport in New Orleans now spun totally out of his control. There was little he could do but react to this woman who embodied everything he'd ever wanted but never dared take. Except here she was and tonight they'd sleep in the same bed. And steps would be taken that couldn't be undone.

She felt small in his embrace. Without the sandals adding to her height he was reminded once again that Jayne, for all her damn-the-torpedoes attitude, was a rather slight woman.

A woman who brought springtime to his lonely soul. And though it might be his downfall, he knew he wasn't going to turn away from her.

He returned her kiss with the passion that had been banked earlier when he'd made that phone call. He told her with his body all the things he'd never say with words. He thrust his tongue deep in her mouth and explored her secrets and let her do the same to him.

She caged his face with her hands, her fingers stroking against the stubble on his chin before slipping to the back of his head to hold him still for her kisses.

She pressed her bosom to his and he felt his chest swell. He put his hands around her waist and lifted her against him, holding her with desperation and need. He gentled the embrace, knowing that if he didn't, he'd either take her standing up right here, or lying down on the sand. Which, despite the way movies portrayed it, would be damn uncomfortable.

''Wow,'' he said, lifting his head.

She smiled at him and his heart melted. He felt too

much and didn't like it, so he hugged her close and tucked her head under his chin. He turned them so that they were looking out over the ocean.

"You know me, boss. When I put my mind to something there's no stopping me."

"Have you set your mind on me?" he asked lightly. But in his soul he felt hope, and it scared him. He was so defenseless where this woman was concerned.

She nodded. "I don't think I have a choice in the matter."

The surf continued to roll over their feet and Jayne looked down at it. "I'm not a big fan of the ocean. I always hated the water," she said.

"I'm the exact opposite. When I was a boy I used to dream of sailing away," he murmured. "Can you swim?"

"I can now. It wasn't fear, it was a real loathing. My mom was always dropping me at school and sailing away to Mexico or the Keys. And to me it represented her leaving."

He took Jayne's hand and led her up the beach. Sinking to the sand, he pulled her between his legs and held her. "Tell me about your childhood."

"Why?"

"Because I want to know you inside out."

Jayne sat there in the moonlight looking like an ethereal creature from another world. He knew that the only way to protect himself would be to learn all he could about this woman. And find a way of exorcising her from his system without forming a deeper attachment.

"This isn't an act for the Angelinis, is it?" she asked, and there was a hint of vulnerability in her voice. Not an Amazon, he reminded himself.

He hugged her closer for a second. Leaning down, he nibbled on the lobe of her ear and dragged his teeth down the side of her neck. Sensual pleasure rippled through her and he pulled her hips tighter against him, arching his back to rub his cock against the curves of her butt.

"What do you think?" he asked.

"Too much is at stake for guessing."

"You're right. I want you, Jayne. I want you for my mistress. No more games or play-acting. I want the real thing." Mentally he knew the impact of this moment was going to be felt for a long time. But one of the first business lessons he'd learned was that some actions were inevitable and the price would have to be paid.

"Me, too. But I want more than just your body."

"Good."

"Good?" she asked. "You know this will impact our working relationship."

"I told you I want to know all your secrets."

"That would leave me with nowhere to hide."

He stroked her face. He'd give anything to be rid of the lust that was running rampant through his body.

No, that wasn't true. As much as he enjoyed Jayne in his office, he knew that he'd enjoy her as a lover even more. And he realized that all these long months when he'd thought he'd done a good job of ignoring her as a woman, he'd been fooling himself. He'd been waiting for her. Waiting for the right moment to do this.

"Don't you think we've done enough hiding?"

Her fingers kneaded his thighs. "Is this an equality thing?"

Instead of answering he pulled her more firmly against him and swept his hands over her, lingering at the full curves of her breasts. Cupping them in his hands and rubbing his palms over their tips until he felt them bud and nestle against him.

Her breath caught in her throat and she shifted against him. He plucked at her nipples and lowered his head, suckling the side of her neck. Her fingers clenched against his thighs and he grew painfully hard. He knew that if he didn't have Jayne soon, he was going to self-combust.

"Let's go back to the room," he said.

"Yes."

Jayne stopped analyzing and just enjoyed being with Adam. She fairly pulsed with need and couldn't wait until they got to their room to make love. She'd seen a very exquisite negligee in her new wardrobe and wanted to see Adam's reaction to her in her gown.

"On a night like this I can easily imagine that pirate Antonio sailing into port here with his beautiful maiden."

Adam's stride was loose and relaxed. It was the first time she'd walked anywhere with him that wasn't at a clipped paced. This was a side to him that she hadn't seen before, and she wanted to explore it more. She wanted to make sure this time on the beach and the magic it wove around her included him, as well.

"I'm sure she wasn't a maiden when they arrived here," he said in a wry tone.

"Unless she was in love with him, I bet she was," Jayne said.

"Don't put too much stock in love, *chère*. Passion would have made her change her mind."

She remembered what he'd said about his father earlier. But she couldn't believe that Adam didn't believe love existed.

All of his relationships were designed to insulate him from feeling anything. The part of her mind that loved puzzles wondered if there were other variables that his mistresses of the past had in common. Physically, she'd noticed they all tended to have long legs and full breasts.

"Passion's overrated. A few pheromones and some scanty clothing are all it takes to evoke passion."

"That's lust," he said.

"Made a study of it, have you?"

He lifted one eyebrow in a very wry expression that made her feel as if she were a naive schoolgirl. She didn't like the feeling, but knew in this instance she was. She didn't have any of his sophistication. To her, sex was more than pheromones, which was why she'd had so few lovers.

"Are you asking me about my love life?" he inquired.

"No. I know you have a revolving door on your bedroom."

He said nothing, but dropped her hand. She stopped and cast her gaze toward him. With one glance she knew he was angry.

"Do you really think so little of me?" he demanded.

Yes and no. Mostly, she was angry at herself for not really understanding what he wanted. "No, I was being flip. I'm sorry. I don't understand why you've chosen only brief affairs."

He tipped his head back and a warm breeze blew around them. The smell of the sea and the night-blooming jasmine surrounded them both, and she wondered how something she'd meant as a nice romantic conversation had gone so wrong.

"Because they are safer," he said softly, his deep voice a whisper on the wind.

"Safer than one-night stands?" she asked, really wanting to understand this complex man.

"No. I can live without sex for a few nights."

"Couldn't prove it by me."

He drew one finger across her collarbone and she shivered at the touch. "That's because you've been a fire in my soul for a long time."

A fire in his soul. The words echoed through her head and her heart. And she threw her arms around him and kissed him. He held her gently and let her control their embrace.

"Thank you for making this sound special."

"It is, Jayne. Don't ever doubt that."

He held her hand loosely and led her toward the path to the hotel. For a moment it felt as if all of her dreams, past and present, melded together. She forgot that she'd been hurt by her father and Ben, and really believed that this time, with Adam, love might stay. Love might blossom. Love might be right.

Anticipation burned through her, making her tremble with desire and a crazy belief that something wrong was being righted. Adam drew her to a halt under a tiki lamp and pulled her close to him. She stretched up on tiptoe to meet his mouth as it descended toward her.

This time it was a sweet embrace with no rushing. It was as if by agreeing that they'd make love in their suite she'd given him permission to linger over her as if she were a gourmet feast.

And he did linger, rubbing his lips sensually against hers until they were so sensitized she couldn't imagine her mouth without his pressed to it. He tilted his head and forced her mouth open, but only filled it with his warm breath.

Pulling back, he glanced down at her with a slight smile, then took her mouth again. He thrust his tongue past her teeth and tasted her deeply. She returned the embrace.

His hands swept up and down her back. Then his left hand slipped around the curve of her waist and caressed her stomach and midriff, working its way slowly up to her breasts. They felt heavy, and she didn't know if she could stand another caress there right now.

But as he cupped her and rubbed his finger around the edge of her nipple, never touching the engorged flesh, she realized that she needed his touch. She whimpered in the back of her throat, wishing for more, needing him to take her nipple between his fingers or even in his mouth.

His lips left hers to slide down her cheek to her neck. He nibbled the column of her throat, then bit gently at the spot where her neck and shoulder met. She arched against him and dug her fingernails into his shoulders through the cloth of his dress shirt.

"*Chère,* I can't wait."

"You don't have to."

He put his hand on the small of her back and pushed her toward the hotel. His pace was definitely quicker now.

"There you two are," Ray said as they reentered the main building. He'd shed his dinner jacket and had the stub of a cigar clamped between his teeth. He took a quick puff on it and then removed the cigar from his mouth.

"Here we are," Adam said.

Angelini must have been standing on the large veranda at the back of the hotel for some time. Jayne tried to determine if Adam had noticed Ray standing there before or after he'd kissed her.

One glance at Adam's face revealed nothing. It was the second time she'd realized that he had an innate ability to hide what he was feeling. She tried not to let the knowledge get to her, like some kind of warning.

"Our jazz band is going to be starting their second set in a minute. I was hoping to catch you on your way back from the walk and change your mind. Want come see them, *compare?*"

"Sure. I want to make some notes on the entertainment. And Jayne likes to dance."

I do? "Not tonight. I've got a headache."

"Are you okay?" Adam asked.

"Yes. I think it was the traveling and the long day at work."

"Well, starting tomorrow you won't have anything to do but relax," Ray said.

"Go ahead, Adam. I'll see you later."

The band started playing and Angelini stood in the

doorway of the hotel. Adam was at a crossroads, one path leading toward the man who held the keys to a deal he wanted to close, and the other leading to Jayne. She tried not to place too much importance on that fact. She also told herself it didn't hurt when he walked away.

Adam was uncomfortable the moment Jayne left. The last thing he wanted to do was spend the evening in a bar with Angelini. The lobby decor hadn't changed in the last twenty years. There was that sixties-style furniture and large paddle fans that kept the air circulating.

Was Jayne okay? She'd seemed fine on the beach a few minutes ago. He would stay for one drink and then make an excuse and leave. The ceiling fan teased his memory and he knew he'd seen it or one like it before.

Ray seemed annoyed when they entered the smoke-filled lounge. The act on the stage was a jazz trio and their music was good, but all Adam saw was Jayne's wide blue eyes filled with a kind of hurt that he hadn't realized he could inflict on another person.

Angelini signaled the waitress when Didi joined them. His wife didn't have much fashion sense. She wore a long skirt in some shade of olive-green. Adam was pained to see a woman dressed so…shabbily. He made a mental note to have the boutique send Didi some new clothes.

"Where's Jayne?"

"Hey, babe. She couldn't join us. Something about a headache."

Didi didn't say anything, but glared at Ray. Those two had the strangest relationship. Adam didn't sense true love between them at all. So he wasn't sure why they were insisting on it from their potential buyers.

"I'll leave you two to discuss business," Didi said with a pointed look at Ray.

"Babe, you're cramping my style," Ray said.

But Didi just walked away. Adam didn't want to sit here and schmooze with Ray for the next thirty minutes. The band slid into an old Miles Davis tune. Adam wished Jayne were here. She'd like this band, and he knew he could coax her onto the small dance floor.

"That one is always sticking her nose in my business. She gives me *agita*. Is Jayne like that?"

"No. Well, sometimes. If I ask her to do something she thinks is ridiculous or not good for business." Adam didn't mind her interference, because nine times out of ten she was right on the money. Jayne had a way of looking at life and situations with clear eyes, and sometimes she saw things that he didn't with his single-minded focus on getting the job done.

"How long you two been together?" Ray asked, taking a sip of his drink.

Adam knocked back his single malt. Not long

enough, he thought. "She started working for me eight months ago."

Ray gave him a man-to-man look. "But you knew you wanted more?"

"What are you, my father confessor?"

"*Madon',* you have no idea. I guess that was pushy."

"Yeah, it was. I know how important it is that a couple buys this place."

"Not any couple," Ray said. "A couple in love."

"Jayne and I are committed to keeping Perla Negra as one of the Caribbean's premiere resorts."

"That's not good enough. I thought I was clear when we spoke on the phone. Perla Negra isn't just a resort. It's a legend."

"Legends make a nice selling point," Adam said.

"Yes, they do," Ray said. He took a puff off his cigar. "But it has to be more than that…. Perla Negra is a place where couples come for romance and to reaffirm the bonds between them."

Perla Negra… The way Ray spoke of it made it seem like something mystical and otherworldly, the perfect place for love. Two things that couldn't survive in the real world, or at least in Adam's world.

"I hate to break it to you, Ray, but some of the couples who come here are adulterers."

Ray shrugged.

Adam knew that not everyone felt the way he did about adultery. He also acknowledged that if his family hadn't been shattered by it he might not hold the act of being unfaithful in such disdain. But he did. And it was the one thing he couldn't forgive or tolerate.

"We provide a place for them to be together. We never stand in the way of true love."

"No matter what kind of mess it leaves behind?" Adam asked.

"I don't follow."

Adam finished off his drink. "Never mind. I think I'd better go see about Jayne."

"No problem," Ray said. "We'll meet you for breakfast on the veranda. I've arranged for you both to take a tour around the island on a boat."

"I can handle the boat myself, so we won't need a guide. Good night."

"Buona notte, compare."

Adam walked through the lobby, intent on getting back to Jayne. Something was wrong and he should have picked up on it earlier instead of letting business distract him. The only reason he had was that business was easier to manage and deal with.

The suite was dark when he entered it except for a small coffee table lamp. He was surprised to see the red file folder sitting in the middle of the desk, the one that held his action items. Jayne must have done some work when she returned to their suite.

Relieved that she must be feeling better—not only because he hoped to persuade her to become his lover—he flipped open the file folder and skimmed the printed e-mails and faxes. Nothing urgent.

He loosened his tie and toed off his shoes as he approached the bedroom. He hadn't worked out the details yet, but he knew he wasn't going to be able to let Jayne leave her job, despite what he'd always believed about lovers working together. He knew that he functioned better when she was around.

He opened the door to the bedroom carefully. Moonlight spilled in from the window, and Adam stayed in the shadows, searching the bed for Jayne's small form. But the bed was empty.

"Chère?"

"Out here," she said. Her voice drifted in from the balcony.

Adam stepped out there, ready to pull her into his arms and finish what they'd started too long ago on the beach. But one look at the way she held herself and he knew something was terribly wrong with Jayne. And it wasn't a damn headache. It was something he'd done.

He suddenly remembered why he preferred having a mistress to actually dating. There was none of this kind of emotional turmoil.

Seven

Jayne had focused on work when she'd returned to their suite. She'd changed out of the wraparound silk skirt—not into the one-of-a-kind negligee that Adam had so thoughtfully provided, but a large T-shirt she'd picked up in the gift shop after Adam had left with Ray.

Jayne realized that the bridge wasn't appearing. She'd leaped off the precipice and had been in a free fall. But she was recovering now. She'd say it was moonlight madness or the sea breeze. A temporary aberration in an otherwise sane person. She and Adam could never be lovers, because she knew without a shadow of a doubt that nothing could ever compete with Powell International in Adam's life. Especially not a lover.

Earlier she'd had some hope in her heart that she could teach Adam to love her, but not anymore.

"Is your head still bothering you?" he asked from the doorway. He was hidden in shadow and she couldn't really see him, just hear his deep, sultry voice. And sense the tension that emanated from him.

An answering tautness sprang to life inside her. She shook her head. "I lied. I didn't have a headache."

He stepped out onto the balcony and leaned next to her at the railing. He crossed his arms over his chest, looking to her like a relaxed man with nothing but time on his hands.

"Why?" he asked. There was a dangerous softness to his tone that she knew from hearing it in the office meant he was close to losing his temper.

She didn't place too much importance on that. She probably should have stayed and acted her role for Ray and Didi, but she couldn't. She'd been exposed there in his arms. And if Adam had been watching her instead of Ray, Jayne feared he'd have seen her heart in her eyes. "I needed to get away."

"From me?"

She nodded. From him and from herself. But there'd been no escaping her own thoughts. So she'd tried to work, and then she'd tried to call her mom, figuring that Mona would know how to keep a man like Adam in her life. But her mother hadn't been home, and in the end Jayne hadn't been able to leave a message.

Adam watched her with an intensity that made her remember his hands on her breasts earlier. She forced her thoughts back to the conversation. "I didn't want to talk to Angelini. I don't think I'm cut out for this, Adam."

"You're talking about becoming my lover."

"At least you didn't say mistress."

He cursed under his breath and pivoted to face the sea, his hands braced on the railing and his head bent. This was the Adam she wanted to wrap in her arms and comfort. Except she knew now the price was too high, and that she wasn't to pay it for a few weeks with him.

"I knew it. What the hell happened?"

How could she explain without revealing her own vulnerability where he was concerned? "I just got a wake-up call."

"Am I supposed to follow that?"

"I guess not. I think the island was working its magic on me. I was falling for the romance of the legend of Perla Negra. And casting you in the role of a swashbuckling hero."

He rested one lean hip against the railing, his expression now forbidding and dark. And she shivered, wrapping her arms around herself.

"But now you've decided I'm not a hero?"

She'd hurt him, she realized. "I think you'd make a wonderful hero, Adam. Just not for me."

"Why not?"

"I need more than you can give me."

"Jayne—"

She reached up and touched his lips to stop the words. "Don't say anything yet. I'm not even sure what I need, but I know it's more than you give your women. And I thought I could make you understand that."

She dropped her hand and tilted her head to study him in the moonlight.

"What happened to change your mind?"

"That kiss with Ray watching. I forgot that even though you want me in your bed, we are playing a part."

"Dammit, Jayne I wasn't playing to Angelini."

She wanted to believe him, but she knew better. Adam was always aware of everyone and everything. "I'm not mad about it. I'd have done the same thing in your position."

"How gracious you are. What if I wanted to make love to you out here on the balcony?"

"I'd have to draw the line there. I just told you I'm having a hard time keeping up with the pretense."

"Exactly what is your difficulty? The hero thing?"

"Yeah, the hero thing."

"There isn't another woman in the world I'd have this conversation with," Adam told her, exasperated.

"Should I be flattered?" she asked mockingly.

"Hell, yes. Dammit, Jayne. For the first time I'm willing to break my own company rules."

"I know. It means something, but not enough. Even though I'm blaming the island resort, that's not what's wrong with me."

"What is it then?"

"I believe in love and want a family. And you don't."

"Would it help if I lied to you?"

"God, no."

"Then I don't know *what* you want. I do know if we both crawl into that bed together the point will be moot."

"Really?"

He raised one eyebrow. "Now who's not being honest?"

Swallowing carefully around her tight throat, she realized that maybe that was why she'd been standing out here waiting for him to return. She wanted to force him to make a decision. And maybe force herself to make one, as well.

"You're right. I guess that's why I left before."

"Don't think about it too much, *chère*. This isn't something either of us is used to or can control."

"It's magic, isn't it, Adam?"

He pulled her into his arms and lowered his head. "You're the magic."

Adam scooped Jayne up in his arms and carried her into the bedroom. Her mouth moved under his with a tentative sweetness he knew was branding him deep in his soul. She let him set the pace, and that was so different from the feisty woman he'd come to know. But he didn't question it.

He set her on her feet and framed her face in his hands. Forcing her head back with the motion of his, he compelled her mouth open. Her tongue greeted his with a tentative foray, but Adam was past the point of foreplay.

He had an erection that was almost painful, and he desperately needed to be inside of Jayne's body. He needed to spread her bare on the bed and then taste every inch of her from head to heels. And only when she'd reached the same fevered pitch that burned through him would he move up over her and claim her as his own.

He left her lips and let his mouth slide down the side of her neck, encountering that thick terry-cloth robe once again. He set her on her feet next to the bed and reached out to turn on the lamp on the nightstand.

He undid the sash at her waist and pulled back the terry cloth, expecting to find her slim, curvy body.

Instead he found a large T-shirt with the resort's logo printed on it.

"What are you wearing?" he asked, the clothing jarring him from the sensual spell he was weaving them both in.

She shrugged. "Something to sleep in."

"I know I ordered a nightgown for you."

"You ordered something for me to wear to bed with a lover."

"Then why aren't you wearing it?" he asked. But in his heart he knew the answer. She'd thought he'd used her to make Ray believe they were a couple. She'd thought he could call passion and interest from his body at will. She'd thought he'd been using her, and she didn't want to be exposed in front of him.

That hurt him in a place he didn't even like to acknowledge he had—his heart. So he ignored that and focused instead on the woman. He would use his skills as a lover to make up for the hurt and pain he'd caused her.

"Why are you making a federal case out of this, honeybun?" she asked in that smart-ass way of hers.

He had to hide a smile because he knew she sassed him only when she was uncertain. And he didn't want Jayne to be unsure of him in the bedroom, or of herself. To his knowledge she hadn't dated anyone in the last eight months since she'd started working for him. He tucked that tidbit away for later.

Right now, he set about seducing her with all the

skill he'd learned since he was a boy on the cusp of manhood. Skills he'd first honed to keep from feeling alone, and then later used so that he didn't have to feel anything other than physical gratification with women. Lately those skills had made him feel jaded. But tonight he was glad for the knowledge, because the only thing that mattered was giving the most pleasure he could to Jayne.

He leaned down, scraping his teeth against the side of her neck and then nibbling at the tender flesh there. Her taste was addictive. Instead he lingered there as if he'd been famished for a long time and she was a full-course meal.

Her hands clutched at his shoulders, fingernails scoring him through the cloth of his shirt. He lifted his head and started unbuttoning it. When he shrugged out of it he felt her appreciative gaze on his body.

"Like what you see?"

"It's okay," she said, and when he started toward her with mock menace, she giggled. Really giggled, and despite the ache in his groin, he felt lighter than ever before.

He scooped her up in his arms and dropped her on the bed. "Let's see if I can change your mind, shall we?"

"It's going to take some work on your part," she said, rolling onto her side and propping her head up on her elbow.

"I'd probably work harder if you showed me a little flesh."

She bit her lip and then lifted the hem of her shirt a little so that it rested on the top of her thighs. "How's this?"

"You've got great legs, *chère.* But…"

She lifted the shirt quickly and flashed him. He had a brief image of a nest of brown, curly hair at the apex of her thighs and a smooth flat stomach. Unless he was mistaken he'd seen a birthmark on her left hip. He reached under the shirt and rubbed the spot.

"What's this?"

"Tattoo," she said.

"Show me?"

"What are *you* going to show *me?*"

"I'm already bare-chested."

"So, convince me," she said.

He sat sideways on the bed, his hips resting next to her stomach. He took her hand from where it gripped the hem of her shirt, bringing it to his mouth. He nibbled the tip of each finger and then kissed the palm of her hand.

He took her hand and stroked it down his body, rubbing her fingers over his sensitive skin. He hardened even more and tried to shift on the bed to relieve some of the pressure between his legs. Damn. He should have removed his pants.

While her hand explored his chest, her fingernails scraped down the center of his body. He lifted her

T-shirt and then bent down to examine her tattoo. It was a pretty little flower that wasn't open, but tightly closed, and a drop of rain lay on the leaf below it.

He traced the pattern with his tongue. Later he'd question her about it, but now he was too close to her body. He could smell the scent of her arousal, and a red mist settled over him. He wanted her, dammit.

He ached to have her.

"Convinced?" he asked, but his voice now was little more than a growl.

She looked up at him from under her lashes. "I'm naked under this shirt."

"Hot damn."

She threw her head back and laughed. He gave up all pretense of playing games, shedding his pants and briefs in one quick motion.

He took the hem of her shirt and pulled it up over her head, tossing it aside. His breath caught in his throat when she lay spread before him in the golden glow of the lamp. She shone with an effervescence he wanted to claim for himself. But he knew at best all he'd have were these moments in her bed.

First Adam caressed her with his eyes and his words. "You're the most exquisite woman I've ever seen."

And when he looked at her the way he was now, she felt as if she really were. For the first time in her life, she didn't feel plain and ordinary. A flush spread over her body and she pushed her shoulders back against the bed, thrusting her breasts into greater prominence.

"Your skin is like the sunrise, warm and golden. And my fingers ache to touch you."

"I ache to be touched," she replied.

He smiled softly in acknowledgment. Then he bent over her, tracing the line of her body with his hands. His touch was so light it felt like a breeze, and she thought she was imagining it. But when he paused to explore her belly button she knew it was real.

He licked a path straight down her center, but when he reached her pubic hair he turned his attention to her thigh, nibbling his way down her left leg and then back up her right.

He avoided the areas of her body that ached most for his contact. Her nipples stood erect waiting for his mouth, but each time he came close he didn't touch them. She writhed on the bed.

He stopped and lingered at her tattoo. With his tongue he traced the pattern again, over and over until she reached down, tunneling her fingers through his hair and holding him to her.

Her tattoo was a big part of who she was—a reminder that she never wanted to be a blossom that had bloomed too many times, like her mother. Jayne had had it done when she was seventeen. It had been painful, but she'd learned that most things in life were.

Adam lifted his head, watching her. He palmed both of her breasts, rubbing their centers in a circular motion until her hips lifted from the bed. His hands moved downward then, skimming her sides and squeezing her hips.

She was helpless to do anything but lie there like a sexual feast prepared for his delight. He stood over her like a god from ancient times. He was like a powerful and successful warrior, she realized, and as she studied him she saw another scar. Unlike the small mark near his nipple, this one ran across his lower belly and down his hip.

She touched the scar gently, tracing over lines that were white with age. He reached down and moved her hand away, bringing her touch instead to his pectorals. How many times had she sat in the boardroom and imagined opening his shirt and touching him?

Now she could. And she did, leaving no area unexplored. She scored his chest with his fingernails when he reached the center of her body, tracing a path with one blunt finger, then dipping inside to test her warmth.

He stretched her carefully, adding a second finger to her opening. She clenched around him, needing more. He bent and she felt the brush of his breath for a second before his tongue tickled her bud.

His fingers moved inside her and his tongue continued its relentless assault until her hips bucked and she grabbed his head, holding him to her hot body.

Her orgasm when it broke over her left her convulsing around him.

Sweat gleamed on her skin and she throbbed from head to toe. She tugged him up over her, skimming her hands down his back. "My turn."

She pushed against him until he was on his back, then knelt next to him on the bed. She kissed him first, exploring that bold, sensual mouth. She could taste herself on him, and it made her feel a little wicked and naughty. And deep in her center she felt an answering pulse.

She scratched his small nipple carefully with her fingernail. He closed his eyes and then reached for her hand, smoothing open her palm and rubbing it over his nipple the way he always caressed her. She watched as his own back arched and his hips jerked toward her.

She took his hard length in her hand. He was hot to her touch and hard. Grasping him at the root, she circled him with her hand and stroked him.

She brought her other arm down and reached between his legs to cup him, squeezing gently until she felt a spurt of moisture at his tip. She rubbed at it with her finger.

Glancing up at him, she realized he was watching her. She lifted her finger to her lips and licked away his taste.

Something primitive lit in his eyes and he rolled over, taking her beneath him. He pinned her to the bed with his hips, his member hot and hard at her entrance. She groaned at the feel of him there and couldn't help thrusting her hips toward him.

He held her still and rubbed his length against her. It felt good, but she was still so empty, and desperately needed him inside her.

With a muttered curse, he pushed away from her. "Are you on the pill?"

She blinked a few times before she understood what he was asking. "Yes."

"Thank God. I hate condoms."

"Me, too," she said. She preferred skin to skin. Especially with Adam.

"I'm healthy," he muttered as he shifted on the bed. He draped her legs over his arms and pushed them back toward her body. "Okay?"

It was way more than okay, but she couldn't speak. He was at her entrance, pushing inside her. He thrust forward until he was fully seated. She relaxed her lower body, trying to take him deeper, and was rewarded when he slipped in farther.

He kissed her, his tongue thrusting into her mouth in the same rhythm as his body took hers. She was on fire and there was little she could do but lay beneath him, an instrument of his pleasure. She'd never had an orgasm more than once in an evening and didn't expect it to be different with Adam.

But then she felt that tingling at the center of her body that signaled one was coming. She gripped

Adam's shoulders, digging her nails into his back as her entire body started to throb and clench around him. When she came this time lights flashed before her eyes, and she felt Adam's body empty into hers at the moment consciousness dimmed.

He roared her name and then continued to thrust a few more times before pulling her into his arms and rolling to his side.

She couldn't think and could barely breathe. But her heart overflowed with emotions and she realized that despite what she'd said earlier at dinner, having a family was no longer her heart's desire. Having Adam in her life forever was.

Eight

Adam woke up alone in bed. The sunlight streamed through the open window and the sound of the surf called him. For a moment he didn't remember where he was, but then the bathroom door creaked open and Jayne tiptoed across the floor.

"Come back to bed, *chère.*"

"In a minute."

She went to the wardrobe and tucked something into one of her drawers. Once again she was wearing that heavy terry-cloth robe. Her lips were still swollen from his kisses and her eyes had a lambent light in them as she gazed at him.

He knew he was existing in a kind of limbo, but

he didn't care. He'd taken Jayne to his bed and it was too late to go back. Hell, he wouldn't even if he could.

Standing next to his side of the bed, she dropped her robe, revealing the naked curves of her body. It was a perfect form, but he'd never been as aroused by just the sight of a woman as he was with Jayne.

Reaching up, he traced her side from her shoulder to her waist, lingering on the tattoo on her hip. Jayne had never struck him as a tattoo person.

"When did you get this?"

"I'll tell you if you take off the sheet," she said.

He was willing to play along. "It had better be a good tale."

"I'll make it worth your while," she said.

There was something about Jayne in this mood that intrigued him. She glowed, though maybe that was from the early morning sun streaming into the room. However, her smile was brighter, and that had nothing to do with Mother Nature. Maybe something to do with him?

He gripped her hips and drew her forward. He didn't want to hurt her. Not that he ever intended to hurt the women in his life, but for some reason he'd never really been able to get things right with females.

Sitting up, he wrapped his arms around her and rested his head against her breast. He heard her heart beating strongly under his ear. His vision was filled with her creamy curves and one pale pink nipple.

"Tell me," he whispered against her flesh. And then watched as her nipple budded and her hands tightened in his hair.

"I got it when I was seventeen."

"Wait," he said. After placing a kiss on her breast, he piled all the pillows behind his back and kicked the sheets to the foot of the bed. Then, grabbing her by the waist, he leaned back, lifting her up over his body. "Now tell me," he said.

"I can't talk now," she said, her voice breathless. She rubbed herself sinuously against him, her warmth sliding over his erection and her nipples brushing his chest.

And he didn't want to talk, either. Later he'd find out the story of why she'd gotten that tattoo and discover the source of that mysterious light inside Jayne. But right now he needed her.

She tipped her head back, bracing her hands on his shoulders, and lifted just the tiniest bit. Sliding his hands between their bodies, he positioned himself.

She opened her eyes and looked right at him. As she slowly sank down on his hard-on. Adam knew he'd never be the same. Her dewy center caressed him like a velvet glove. She paused once he was fully sheathed, and squeezed him with her inner muscles.

When he groaned her name, she smiled. She relished her power over him. "Like hearing me moan?"

She bit her bottom lip as he took her breasts in his hands, pinching her nipples carefully and then scraping them with his thumbnails. She moaned and her hips flexed against his. He soothed the small pain with his palm before angling his head and sucking one nipple into his mouth.

Her hands left his shoulders to hold his head to her. She rocked slowly over him and he knew she wasn't torturing him this time, but simply lost in the sensations he was calling forth.

"Moan for me," he said against her skin, nibbling his way to her other nipple and suckling there.

"Not yet," she said, and pushed him back against the pillows. She braced her hands against his chest, nails scoring his skin mildly. And she lifted herself off of him. She let him slide all the way out of her body, and paused while he hovered at her entrance.

He wanted to let her run the show, but enough was enough. Adam yearned for her with a desperation he would never acknowledge. He longed to once again bathe in her warmth and forget about the hunger that had been festering in him for too long.

Wrapping one arm around her, he thrust upward with his hips, then rolled them both over so that she was under him.

"Hey, I was in charge," she said, but her eyes drifted closed as he started thrusting inside her.

When her back arched to receive each of his thrusts, the slim expanse of her neck was revealed and he lowered his head to suckle at the point where her collarbone met it.

Her hands moved up and down his back. She clenched him with her muscles deep inside every time he retreated, and from her mouth came a litany that was his name.

Stroking her back, he took the full curves of her butt in his hands and caressed the crease. She arched toward him, seeking her release. With a thousand electric sparks, Adam felt his own climax sweep over him in one continuous wave, and after that he couldn't move. Lowering his head, he rested it on her chest and held her. She clutched him to her breast and didn't say a word. But Adam knew that something had happened between them and that the world outside had changed for them, as well.

They'd both drifted back to sleep after their early morning lovemaking, and in her dreams, Jayne had never had to let Adam go. He woke her the second time with a sweet kiss and a joining that was so deep and forceful that she felt certain he'd branded her soul. Once their heartbeats had settled down, he'd urged her into the shower, promising her a surprise.

The craft that Ray and Didi had provided was a high-speed motorboat. Adam was like a kid with a new toy. He raced it into the surf away from the island, doing tight turns and making sea mist spray over them both.

And Jayne was definitely surprised. Adam seemed years younger out here. He was more at home on the ocean than anyplace she'd observed him. This seemed a more natural side of him.

He was wearing his swim trunks and sunglasses, his head tipped back to the sunshine. She wore only her bikini, because once they'd left the marina, Adam had refused to allow her to wear the cover-up she'd brought.

Neither of them had discussed the future or her position within Powell International, and Jayne wasn't sure how to plan her next step. So she was doing something decidedly un-Jayne and ignoring the urge to make a plan around this. Because if she started planning it would mean that she'd given up on the fantasy of making him fall in love with her.

And after last night it was clear to her that she had no other goal. She scanned his strong, muscled body, watching him control the vessel and remembering his hands on her body.

"Why are you staring at me?"

She blushed and he raised one eyebrow, then slowed the boat. She was sitting in the captain's chair and Adam stood next to her, his powerful legs braced as he maneuvered across the water.

"You seem very at home on the ocean," she said at last.

He shrugged. "I am."

"Still dreaming of sailing away?" she asked lightly, remembering what he'd said on the beach.

And she wondered if he dreamed of doing so alone or if now she was there with him.

"Sometimes."

"Now?"

He shook his head. "Not with you at my side. Want to try piloting the boat?"

"No," she said.

"Chicken."

"Ha. I'm not scared to learn how to drive this boat."

"Prove it."

"I don't have to prove it. I'm too self-confident to rise to your bait."

"What if something happens to me and you have to find your way back on your own?"

"I brought my cell phone."

He killed the engine, dropped the anchor and spread his arms wide, and she couldn't help but imagine him as Poseidon, king of all he surveyed. "There's something about being at sea."

"Yeah, fish smells and motion sickness."

He rested his hips against the railing of the boat and crossed his ankles. "The next time some woman tells me I'm not romantic…"

Jayne tried to laugh, but the thought of him with another woman wasn't a comfortable one. So she forced her mind away from that. Instead she stood and smiled sweetly at him before pushing him overboard.

He came neatly to the surface. "Oh, you're going to pay for that."

"Is the boat safe here?"

"Yes, my practical Jayne, it is."

"Good." She dived overboard, bobbing up next to him. She'd no sooner surfaced then she felt his hand on her thigh, strong sure fingers slipping under her suit to caress her. She stopped treading water for a minute and he gave her a wicked grin before tugging her under.

That dirty dog, distracting her with sex! They played a rough-and-tumble game of dousing each other, but each brush of his body against hers made her want him locked deep inside her again.

After twenty minutes had passed, she surfaced and glanced around to find Adam. When he reappeared, she swam behind him, wrapped her arms around him and whispered the most deliciously sexual things in his ear until he grabbed her wrist and hauled her back to the boat.

As soon as he got them both out of the water, he laid her down on the bench seat at the back of the cruiser. "Get naked."

He stripped off his own swimsuit and watched her. She'd shed her top but was still struggling out of her bottoms. He reached for the fabric and tugged it down her legs. Then he lowered himself to her, kissing her as he slid deep inside. She wrapped her legs around his hips and held on to him. "Talk dirty to me again, *chère*," he murmured.

She did, telling him in explicit detail what he did to her and what she wanted to do to him. Her words lit a raging fire inside Adam. Their coupling was fast and furious.

In the aftermath, she clung tightly to him, her mouth resting on his chest. He tasted faintly of the sea and of man.

He cradled her in his strong arms, slipping one of his thighs between hers. One hand cupped her breast and the other her hip. The boat rocked them gently and the sea breeze cooled their flushed bodies.

"I don't want to sail away. I'm enjoying myself too much."

"Me, too," she confessed.

He drew his finger down her cheek and under her chin, tilting her head back for his kiss. He lingered over her mouth for a few minutes and when he lifted his head she wanted to pull him back to her.

"I'm glad. Did you bring that treasure map?"

"Ray gave us one as we were leaving. Are we going hunting for our heart's desire?"

Something warm lit his eyes, and though she knew it wasn't practical and made no sense, she couldn't help thinking that Adam had found what he'd been searching for in her.

Adam and Jayne dropped anchor in a small cove. He took ashore the picnic lunch that the hotel staff had provided and then returned to carry Jayne to the beach.

He should've stayed in the boat and continued to survey the island from the sea. He should be checking on neighboring property that might be available for sale. He should be concentrating on work, but he didn't want to.

"I could have walked."

"I know," he said. His arms felt empty without her, but he didn't tell Jayne that. He had the feeling she saw too much, anyway. He set her on her feet and together they spread out the blanket and food. Because Adam didn't believe in drinking and driving—even a boat—he didn't drink any of the wine that was in the cooler.

Jayne was careful to steer the conversation away from personal topics and onto current events, which they both shared similar views of, and movies, which they didn't. The sappier the storyline, the more Jayne liked it. And she wasn't above arguing with him to make a point.

There was a gleam in her eyes as she asked him about his favorite book. Though he liked true crime and biographies, he didn't want to debate his personal choices anymore.

"*Lord of the Rings,*" he said.

"Finally. I thought we had nothing in common."

"I can't believe you like those books, Jayne. They aren't sappy enough."

"You're in trouble now, honeybun."

"I'm scared," he said.

She dived for Adam, mercilessly tickling him. They wrestled on the blankets until somehow she ended up under him. Then he couldn't resist lowering his head and kissing her mouth. The fact that he had rights to her seductive lips pleased him.

He lifted his head after long moments and then sat up.

"Adam?"

"I want to know more about you," he murmured.

"What do you want to know?" she asked. Jayne sat up in turn, leaning back on her elbows.

He traced the bottom edge of her tattoo with his finger. "You never told me about this. You said you got it when you were seventeen. Why?" He'd never noticed until now that there was a core of herself that Jayne kept hidden. Adam had the feeling she was dancing just out of his reach, and that no matter how many times he claimed her body, part of her soul remained untouched. But she'd scored him deeply with her presence in his life and he wouldn't tolerate not affecting her as strongly.

"My mom has one similar to it. But it's a fully open flower."

"Why isn't yours?"

"I've always wanted to be her opposite."

Adam tugged the side of her suit down so that he could see the entire design again. There was something very restrained about Jayne's tattoo. "Tell me about your mom."

"She's sophisticated and chic. She always has the hottest new car. She's well traveled and speaks three languages fluently."

"Is she American?"

"Yes, but her father was from Colombia. She started modeling when she was fourteen."

"Do you look like her?"

"I have her eyes and that's about it. She towers over me and she's very voluptuous."

"Then you get these from her, as well," he said, cupping her full breasts.

Jayne batted his hands away playfully. "I guess. We don't really have that much in common."

"Why not?"

"She is a rich man's mistress."

"Are you sure it's not a relationship?"

"Very. She's living with Hans for six months. It's her standard arrangement. You have that in common with her."

"My arrangements usually don't have a time limit," he said. He tried to imagine what kind of upbringing that would be for a child. Especially one as sensitive as Jayne.

Adam stood and seated himself behind her. Wrapping his arms around her waist, he pulled her back against his chest. ''What about your dad?''

''I don't know him.''

Her neck was tempting him once again. It was long and slim and very elegant, and she tasted sweeter there than anywhere else. Did she really? he wondered. Deciding to test his theory, he bent and nibbled at her shoulder.

''Does he know about you?'' Adam asked. It was one of his fears, and why he was also so careful when he slept with a woman. The thought of having a child out there he didn't know about made his gut clench.

He didn't particularly want kids, which was why he had short-term affairs. He knew that children needed a father who'd love and protect them, a dad who would dedicate himself to his family. Adam had dedicated himself to business and a quest for vengeance against a man who was no longer alive.

''My mother left him before I was born. I saw him only once.''

She shuddered in his arms and Adam tightened his grip around her, wanting to protect her from painful memories. ''What was that like?''

''You don't want to know.''

''Of course I do,'' he said. He didn't understand it, but he needed to know everything about her.

''I…I hid in my closet. And he tried to talk to me but I wouldn't come out.'' She rubbed her arms, because she couldn't seem to stop shaking all of a sudden.

"I'm sorry."

"Don't be. I was a mistake neither he nor my mother had anticipated."

"Someone called you a mistake?"

"Not in so many words. But I felt like it."

He lowered them both to the blanket. Curling himself around her, he carefully made love to her, trying to erase the memories of her childhood with his body. He knew in his heart that any kind of relationship that he might propose would be intolerable to Jayne. She needed a man who could commit himself to her and brand her with his name and his ring.

Adam refused to acknowledge the desperation in his actions as he brought Jayne to one shattering climax after another. He found he was sated himself only when she was covered with sweat and calling his name in a hoarse voice.

And after his own orgasm ripped through him, leaving him shattered and weak, he cradled her close to his body and prayed for something he couldn't put into words.

Nine

Adam docked the boat smoothly that afternoon. Ray waited for them in the marina lounge. The rotund little man smiled when he saw them and offered Adam a cigar.

"Go ahead, Adam. I want to try my hand at the treasure map, now," Jayne told him.

"I'll go with you."

"Are you sure?" she asked. The Adam she'd come to know as her boss would never pass up an opportunity to meet with a prospective buyer.

"Yes," he said, and there was a conviction in his expression that warmed her heart.

Ray waved them off, and Adam took her hand. He

led her up the path toward a cave in the hills where the treasure of La Perla Negra supposedly resided.

"Why are you doing this? I know you don't care about the treasure," Jayne stated.

"Maybe you don't know me as well as you think you do."

"That's doubtful. After all, I've been overseeing your office for almost a year now. I think I know the kind of man you are."

"What kind am I?"

She wanted to keep things light, but every action that Adam had taken today had been something out of a dream. No, not a dream—her secret desires. The romantic picnic and their lovemaking had made her feel as if there was hope. That her love for Adam wasn't necessarily one-sided and that the future might hold more for them than she'd ever dared imagine.

"You like the finer things in life."

"True. What else?"

"You're very determined and stubborn."

"Not that you share that trait."

"Be quiet. I'm the one talking here."

"Sorry, *chère*. What else were you going to say?"

"I think you might be lonely and that you've found a way to disguise that from the world. Those gorgeous mistresses of yours give you the illusion that you have a successful life."

He stopped on the path, dropping her hand. She

wondered if she'd gone too far. But then he cupped her face and lowered his head, sipping at her lips as if they were a fine wine.

"You're right. But I have my reasons," he whispered.

"What are they?"

"I don't want to ruin any illusions you might have of me."

"You won't," she said. Nothing could dim the love she felt for Adam. It was strange to think that when they'd left New Orleans he'd been her fantasy lover, and now he was the real thing.

He led her to a wrought-iron bench facing the resort, and beyond it, the ocean. "When I was fourteen my dad ran off with his secretary, leaving Mom and me on our own."

That explained Powell International's policy against workplace romances. Jayne wondered if Adam even realized he was trying to protect the families of all his employees from the same hurt he'd endured. Did he realize he couldn't?

"That must have been hard," she said.

He shrugged. "Mom had never worked a day in her life and was totally lost. She locked herself in her room and cried for three months. I took a job at a fast-food joint and started working to support us.

"I made a vow, Jayne, to never hurt anyone the way my mom was hurt."

Jayne slipped her arm around his waist and held him tightly. "What about you? Didn't your father's leaving hurt you?"

"No. I was almost a man. Strong enough to stand on my own."

But Jayne sensed he hadn't been. For all his demanding nature at work, Adam was still an extremely fair boss. He valued his workers and took a personal interest in their lives, especially those on his executive staff.

"Fourteen's still a boy," she said.

He hugged her close to his side. "You sound so fierce. Going to beat up everyone who's hurt me?"

"If I could."

"Oh, Jaynie. Don't care too deeply about me. I don't think I could endure hurting you."

"Because I care so deeply, you won't."

"I will. I'm not meant for…happily ever after."

"That's crap. Everyone is meant for bliss. You're just afraid because your parents' relationship went sour."

"Everyone? I don't see Mr. Right in your life."

She pinched him because he'd angered her. He was Mr. Right, and if he'd just open his eyes he'd see it.

"Ouch," he said, rubbing his side.

"Come on. Let's find that treasure."

She started down the path, trying to gain control over her emotions. Adam grabbed her arm, stopping her.

"I didn't mean it that way. I just…I've tried marriage before."

"I didn't know that."

"Not many people do. She left me for a man she worked with. We'd only been married six months."

"Oh, Adam," Jayne said.

"Don't pity me. I expected it to happen and it did. Modern people aren't meant for marriage. It's an institution that's outdated."

"You don't really believe that. You're just lashing out."

"What are you, an amateur shrink?"

"Ha! You know it's true. I have a hard time with relationships because of my mom. And because I'd never talk to my dad. I wanted to, you know?"

"Why didn't you?"

"I was so afraid of him. I figured he'd left before my birth because he didn't want me. And I was so scared that once he saw me he'd remember that and leave."

Adam tightened his arm around her. He muttered something under his breath that she couldn't understand, but she felt safer than she ever had before. And a certainty that they were meant to be together.

They found the treasure chest just inside the cave. Inside were polished stones carved with the resort's logo. There was an incantation on the wall that visitors were supposed to repeat for the next three days after being at the cave, and then they'd find their heart's desire.

Jayne reached for a stone and then pivoted to face Adam. "Aren't you taking one?"

"No. I don't believe in all that mumbo jumbo."

"This from the man who has a voodoo doll on his desk."

"That's a joke and you know it."

"Yeah, sure it is. That's why if someone moves it from the right corner you have a fit."

"A fit? Jayne, men don't have fits."

"What do they have?"

"Nothing but a desire for perfection and a well-ordered life. My office is my domain and as such everything in there shouldn't be touched."

"Was that a royal decree? Should I send that in memo form to the staff?"

"No, Miss Sassy Mouth. You're the only one who thinks she can charge around in my life and make changes."

"Well, someone has to. You're stuck in a rut."

Not anymore. He didn't know if he should thank Jayne or curse her, but she'd definitely upset his routine. "What are you wishing for?"

"We're not supposed to tell," she said. Then closed her eyes and made her wish.

She then read three times the incantation that was printed on the wall, as the instructions said.

"Aren't you supposed to spin around and spit on the floor next? Say some word like *abracadabra?*"

"Don't scoff at me," she said. She moved away from the chest toward the back of the cave, stopping in front of the display area, which held a table and chairs. Next to it was a canopy bed with heavy velvet drapes. According to the legend, the pirate and his bride had lived in the cave while building their home.

Adam took a stone when Jayne wasn't looking and slipped it into his pocket, feeling like an idiot the entire time, but unable to stop himself. He wanted Jayne to stay with him even after they returned to their real world. And he'd do anything to make it happen—even wish on a stone.

He knew that asking her to be his mistress wasn't an option. There was no way she'd ever agree to it. Adam was honest enough to admit he wouldn't really be happy unless she held a more permanent position in his life.

He was going to ask her to move in with him and be his lover. In his mind there was a distinction. He'd ask her to live with him and, most of all, he'd allow her to still work with him at Powell.

"I wonder what it was like living here back then."

"Kind of damp and moldy."

"That sounds so romantic, Adam. Frankly, I expected better from you. Aren't you the man who is known for his candlelight dinners?"

"Candlelight is one thing. Living in a cave is something else. Don't tell me you'd be happy here."

"If I was with a man who loved me, who risked everything for me, I think I would be."

"Is that what you wished for?" he asked, hoping she hadn't. Because of all the things he could give her, love wasn't one of them. He'd always been afraid to trust in love because every example he'd seen had left destruction in its path.

"I'm not supposed to tell anyone," she repeated, turning aside. Adam knew she was hiding from him, but he let it go.

"I wish I'd paid more attention in school to geology," she continued. "This cave is fascinating."

"What do you want to know?" he asked, walking over to her. There was a small pool in the center of the cave. The Angelinis had done a decent job of making the grotto look like a spot where a pirate would leave his lost treasure. They had flickering sconces on the rock walls and the stones were kept in a carved wooden chest.

"What are those?" she asked.

"Stalagmites?"

"You didn't pay attention in school, either?"

"I usually sat in the back of the class and slept."

"How did you get into college?"

"A lot of hard work. I flunked out of high school and realized that the kind of success I wanted wouldn't come from working in restaurant management. So I studied and took the GED. My mom started coming out of her shock by then and we sold real estate. That combined with my earnings from drag racing gave us a financial base. When I had enough money, I went to college.''

''Where's your mom now?'' Jayne asked after a few minutes. He knew Jayne well enough to recognize that she was organizing facts and forming opinions. She always did an inordinate amount of research.

''Living in Tucson with her second husband, Al. They retired there four years ago.''

''Arizona is next on my list of states to visit. What about your dad and the secretary? Where do they live?''

Everyone knew about Jayne's fifty states. In her office she had a big map of the U.S. and she'd put a smiley face sticker on the ones she'd been to.

She'd asked about his dad. Adam wanted to ignore the fact that he had a father, even though in his mind he saw the two of them playing football in the backyard of that big old house where they'd lived outside of New Orleans when he was a boy.

''Adam? What about your dad?''

''He died in a plane crash.''

''I'm sorry.''

''It didn't matter,'' he said. He didn't tell her that the crash had happened when his dad was returning from this resort with his secretary. Adam would never let Jayne know the devastating sense of loss he'd experienced when he'd learned his dad had died. And then three days later, when they'd received the letter he'd sent them saying he was running off with Martha.

Jayne slipped her hand into his, and he felt the rock in her palm, warm from her skin. "What are you doing?"

She closed her eyes for a moment. "I'm sharing my heart's desire with you."

"Even though I scoffed at you."

"Yes. I don't want to be happy if you're not."

His gut tightened and he felt weak in a way that wasn't physical. His heart raced and he realized that he had the power to hurt Jayne. Not just because of the habits ingrained from a lifetime spent not forming attachments. But because she had a soft side under her modern exterior, and he was the man she'd let see it.

"I have to make a few phone calls before dinner. Would you do me a favor?" Adam asked when they returned to their suite a few hours later.

"What kind of favor?" she asked. She was pleasantly tired from walking and being in the sun all day.

"A charity mission. Didi Angelini has the worst taste in clothes of any woman I ever met. I think that might be part of the problem between her and Ray."

Ray did have a bit of a roving eye, and there was

a strange sort of tension between the two of them. "I noticed he can't keep his eyes off the island women."

"Me, too." Adam reached into his back pocket and took out his wallet. He pulled out his platinum card and handed it to her. "Get her a totally new wardrobe on me."

"Why are you doing this?" Jayne asked. Not that she minded the task. She just wanted to understand this facet of the man she loved. He was always unfailingly polite to women, and though he only involved some in his life as mistresses, he seemed rather protective of the women he knew.

"I can't stand to see a woman in an ugly dress," he said, going to the fax machine and sorting through the papers piled there.

"I'm not buying it, stud muffin. Tell me why."

"Jayne," he asked, as if bored with the conversation, "do you really want me to spank you?"

He stepped toward her with mock aggression, and it was all she could do not to throw her arms open and say, *take me, big boy.* But she knew Adam wasn't above using sex to distract her, and she wanted to know why this was important to him.

"Yes, but not now. I want to know why. You've done this two other times that I know about, and as far as habits go, this is a fairly odd one."

He stopped halfway toward her and thrust his hands into the pockets of his pants. His gray eyes were cold and steely, and she had the feeling if she didn't handle this properly he'd clam up.

"I don't want any lip about this," he warned her.

"I won't give you any. I'm just curious. I want to know more about what makes Adam Powell tick."

"Guilt, greed and lust make me tick," he said, self-derision lacing his words.

"There's more to you than that."

He shrugged. "Some days it doesn't feel like it."

"Stop trying to distract me."

Finally he looked up at her. "It sounds stupid when I say it out loud."

She closed the gap between them. Wrapping her arms around his ribs, she nestled her head right over his heart, and listened to its slow, calming rhythm.

"Whisper it to me."

He said her name and closed his hands over her shoulders. Tipping her face up to his, he dropped one small kiss on her lips. His erection nudged against her stomach and she knew he wanted her. But she also knew that he was hiding something.

"I want you, stud muffin, but I want answers, too."

"God, Jayne, if you call me that in front of anyone I really will turn you over my knee."

"Promises, promises. The clothing?"

He lifted her in his arms and carried her to one of the overstuffed chairs in the living area, where he sank down and settled her on his lap. Then he tucked her head under his chin. She tried to move so she could see him, make eye contact, but he was having none of it.

"My mom had the worst sense of style. One of the reasons my dad left us was that he was embarrassed by her. My mom had no idea how to change that about herself, and frankly, I didn't either. Then I met Susan. She was very fashionable and knew how to dress right. So Mom picked up a few tips from her."

"Who's Susan?" Jayne asked. He'd never talked about that time in his life before and she had a hard time picturing Adam as anything but the successful CEO he was today.

"She was my wife."

Jayne still had a hard time coming to terms with Adam as married. It didn't fit with the man she'd come to know. Even in her wildest dreams she didn't picture the two of them married.

She ached to wrap her arms around him but couldn't because of the way he held her so tightly.

"How old were you? You didn't say before."

"Twenty when we married. Twenty-one when she left. The only good thing she did was help Mom with her sense of style. After that if I saw a woman whose marriage was on the rocks and her clothing wasn't exactly fashionable, I'd help out."

"You can't fix everyone's marriage."

"I'm not even trying."

"Then what are you doing?"

"Leveling the playing field."

"That is one of the—"

"Don't say it. I warned you."

"—sweetest things I've ever heard."

"Oh, God, give me a break. I also can't stand to see a woman hiding from her natural sensuality."

"Damn, why didn't you say so earlier?"

He cupped her chin and lifted her toward him for a long, lingering kiss—at first just the soft brushing of lips against lips. Then Adam angled his head and let his tongue slowly enter her mouth, tasting her deeply.

When he lifted his head, there was more than just lust in his eyes. She saw affection and caring and a slew of other emotions she'd never expected to see when Adam looked at her.

"I *have* to call Sam this afternoon," he said at last.

"Apparently I have some shopping to do," Jayne replied, getting to her feet.

"I'll be done in thirty minutes," he said.

"No, you won't. You can't get Sam off the phone in less than forty-five."

"If I had the right incentive I could."

"I'll see what I can do."

He stopped her halfway to the door, kissing her again. This time it wasn't the sweet lingering embrace of earlier. His hands cupped her butt and he drew her hard against him. His mouth ravaged hers.

When he set her back on her feet she felt as if she'd

just lived through a class IV hurricane. "What was that?"

"Incentive for you," he said with a wink, steering her toward the door.

Jayne walked out of their room and paused for a minute on the gravel path. Adam was changing. He was no longer the unemotional man she'd worked for a few days earlier, and though she knew it might be foolhardy, her heart beat a little faster at the thought of why he'd changed.

Ten

"**W**here are the women?" Ray clamped the butt of a cigar between his teeth and glanced around the room. He checked his watch one more time and then scowled.

Adam wasn't concerned. Jayne had called earlier and said that she and Didi would meet them at the restaurant. He'd missed her while he'd been working. Sam, his vice president, hadn't been expecting a call, but Adam had needed some space from Jayne.

He'd told her things he'd never meant to reveal. He had a lot of difficulty keeping her in the neatly labeled slot he'd assigned her to.

They were dining in the small town at a chef-owned restaurant that Jayne had discovered when she'd researched the island. She'd suggested Adam check it out and maybe hire the chef for the resort's restaurant. As charming as Perla Negra was, it lacked the amenities guests of Powell International were used to.

"Relax. Jayne is the most organized person I know. They'll be here in time for our reservation."

"You're right, *compare*. Jayne's a firecracker."

"She is. I'm lucky to have her. Didi's not exactly a slouch, either."

"That one likes to make my life uncomfortable," Ray said.

"I think women are meant to do that to a man."

"Makes life damn disturbing," Ray said. His mouth fell open and he dropped his cigar. Adam glanced over his shoulder and felt his own jaw sag. Jayne and Didi stood in the doorway.

Ray muttered something in Italian that Adam couldn't understand, but the sentiment was one he shared. The women both looked breathtaking. Jayne's eyes sparkled when they met his and he couldn't help smiling back at her. Didi was finally wearing something that wasn't butt-ugly and actually fit her body.

But Adam couldn't take his eyes off of Jayne. It scared him to realize how important she was to him and to his life. He couldn't take the risk of letting her be that vital, and he wondered for a second if he shouldn't just distance himself from her now.

Actually, he didn't think he could.

Didi started to look a little apprehensive, and crossed her arms over her chest. Jayne gestured for her to drop her arms to her sides, which the other woman did.

"Well, aren't you going to say anything?" Jayne demanded.

Adam recovered first and crossed to the ladies. He took Didi's hand in his and brushed a kiss against the back of it. "You look beautiful. Ray and I are going to be the envy of every man in the place tonight."

Then he turned to Jayne, and smooth words deserted him. He pulled her close and kissed her fiercely, needing her with a desperation that made his soul wary. When he lifted his head, her made-for-sin mouth was dewy and swollen from his kisses. Adam wanted to say the hell with dinner and retreat back to their room.

"Babe...I...you..." For the first time since they met Ray was almost speechless.

"Cat got your tongue, Ray?"

"You look nice. I think our table is ready."

"It's a wonder you're any good at your job," Didi said.

Ray wrapped his arm around Didi's waist and led her toward the hostess stand. Adam and Jayne followed, listening to the bickering couple.

"I'm much better at it when I don't have you sticking your nose in my business."

"Babe," Didi said in a good imitation of the way Ray always said it. "I'm not sticking my nose in, I'm making sure you do things properly."

Luckily, they soon reached the table and were seated. It was one of the best in the house, in front of a large open window that let in warm sea breezes and had a view of the ocean equaled by none. Adam kept his hand on Jayne's back even after she sat down. He liked the feel of her silky smooth skin.

He also liked the fact that he had the right to touch her. That Jayne belonged to him. And dammit, she did belong to him, in a way no person ever had before. He shuddered a little as he realized it was too late to guard against caring for her. He already did.

Their waiter was a young Jamaican man with a smile a little too friendly when he turned it on Jayne. Adam leaned over and kissed her mouth in a way that told the world she belonged to him. Then he calmly ordered for both of them.

Jayne pinched his leg under the table and he reached over to her thigh and caressed it. Ray and Didi excused themselves to talk to a couple who were staying at the resort.

"What was that about?"

"What?" Adam took a sip of his drink, continuing to caress Jayne's leg under the table.

"That male territory thing you did. Why don't you get out a Sharpie pen and write your name on my forehead?"

"You'd let me do that?" he asked.

"You're hopeless," she said with a laugh.

"Only where you're concerned."

Her breath caught and she looked up at him with...
Oh, God, don't let it be love in her eyes. His heart
speeded up and he knew the situation was quickly
spinning out of his control.

A small band took the stage and soon the sounds
of reggae and calypso music filled the joint. Adam
watched Jayne humming along under her breath and
swaying to the music.

"Want to dance?"

"Yes, but you need to talk to the chef and then I
think you should—"

He quieted her by sliding his hand down her neck
to her collarbone and holding her carefully. "Come
on," he said, tugging her to her feet. "It's been too
long since I held you."

She said nothing as he led her to the dance floor
and pulled her into his arms. She nestled there trust-
ingly, laying her head on his heart as she always did,
and he prayed that she couldn't hear its frantic beating.

The rest of the week flew by and Jayne spent every
hour of the day with Adam, learning more about him.
She realized he loved to be on the water and had
rented a sailboat for them to use every afternoon.
She'd always known that he was intensely private and

very driven, but on the island she learned why. She thought she finally understood why he limited himself to relationships that were clearly defined. He wanted to protect everyone involved.

She'd never have guessed the man who was ruthless in the boardroom and who was known as a shark in the hotel world would have a hidden depth of caring that would make her heart ache.

Today he was on the beach playing a game of coed volleyball with a group of singles that had come to the resort looking for some fun. Adam had been casually studying the resort demographics. She knew because she'd spent as much time at her computer, making charts and graphs and compiling reports, as she had with Adam.

But she didn't mind it. In fact, she found that their relationship had added a dimension to their work life that she hadn't expected.

He valued her opinion, and he took breaks more frequently now just to sit quietly with Jayne. Sometimes they'd go for a walk, other times she'd tease him by calling him stud muffin and he'd fall on her, making love to her with a fierceness that convinced her he must love her.

Adam planned to take the charming resort and make it into an all-inclusive vacation destination for families. She'd just concluded a call with a treasure hunter who'd agreed to redesign the treasure map.

Ray had all but said that Adam could purchase La Perla Negra.

Jayne thought that might be why Adam looked so relaxed today. She sat on the sidelines, watching him play. He was bare-chested and sweaty, and when he looked at her she felt the intensity of his gaze even from beneath those dark sunglasses of his.

The game broke up. Adam perched on the arm of her chair and took a sip of her margarita. "Where were you?"

"Talking to Guy O'Bannon."

Adam raised one eyebrow in question.

"The treasure hunter."

"What kind of name is Guy O'Bannon?"

Jayne shrugged. "I think he made it up. He was funny as anything. I made arrangements for him to come down to the island. For a fee he'll redesign the treasure hunt and add some false trails as well as help us with the legend."

"Great. Now all I need is for Ray to sign that contract and everything will be in place."

Adam signaled the waitress and ordered a Corona. Then he lifted her from the chair. He took her place and settled her on his lap, curving his hand around her waist and caressing her with languid strokes of his fingers. "I like this place. I never expected to."

"Why not?" she asked, trying to focus on the conversation and not the delicious tingles spreading over her body. She rested her head on his shoulder and wished that this special closeness never had to end.

"This is the resort that my dad brought his secretary to when he left us."

"Oh, Adam." She tried to turn to face him but he held her tightly in his arms. Then he leaned down to glare at her.

"Don't say my name like that. I'm not a broken-hearted fourteen-year-old."

"I never thought you were. It's just... I wish you never had to suffer," she said, speaking from the heart. She knew that there was no way to protect Adam from being hurt, and to even think that this strong man needed her protection was almost ridiculous. But it didn't change the way she felt.

"At least I had my dad for those fourteen years. I'd forgotten all the good memories for a long time," Adam said at last. He cupped her face, tilting it back so he could sip from her lips. She tasted of salt and lime from her margarita.

His fingers feathered over her skin, as light as the sea breeze, and her body responded. She would never get enough of him. She'd stopped thinking that they would ever be apart, because it was too painful to imagine a time when he wasn't in her life. He owned her, body, heart and soul, and she suspected sometimes that he knew it. It didn't really bother her because she felt as if she was coming to own him in the same way.

He lifted his head, his lips wet from her kisses, and his eyes narrowed. Under her buttocks she felt him hardening. She had the feeling they weren't going to be sitting in the sun for too much longer. But anticipation was exquisite, and she knew he felt the same when he rubbed his hard-on against her and then leaned back against the chair.

She cast around for something to distract them. "How do you feel about your dad now?"

"I can't forgive him, Jayne, and I don't think I ever will be able to. But at least now I can remember the good times before."

"I'm glad. Childhood should leave lots of good, lasting memories."

He opened his eyes and she smiled up at him. "You sound like a sappy old greeting card," he murmured.

She knew she'd gotten too close with her probing, and didn't want to back down, but knew she had to. "Yeah, you bring that out in me, stud muffin."

"I thought I warned you not to call me that," he growled.

"Don't get all bristly. Here comes your beer."

"I'll take it with me."

"Oh? Where are you going?"

"Back to our room, to paddle that sweet backside of yours."

"I don't think so."

"Then you should have been paying attention."

Adam lifted her against his chest and stood up. ''Be a good girl, Jayne, and grab my beer.''

A river of anticipation swelled inside her. She didn't fear him and knew he'd never hurt her. So she reached for his beer and cradled the cold bottle against her stomach while she signed their tab with one hand. Adam walked up the path to their room with sure steps. And Jayne knew in her heart that she and Adam were going to be together forever.

Adam had Jayne open the door of their suite, and walked into the sun-filled room. He wasn't seriously thinking of spanking her, though with her sassy mouth she'd tempted him more than once to turn her over his knee. What he wanted more than anything was to make love to Jayne. Their time at the resort had been the most ideal fantasy of his life, and at the same time the most tense.

He knew it couldn't last and was afraid for the first time that he wouldn't be able to manage this properly. That somehow Jayne would slip through his fingers and his life would once again be filled with cold beauties instead of the fire that Jayne brought to his soul.

Adam walked into the bedroom. The drapes were drawn and only a little dappled light filled the room. He settled Jayne on the edge of the bed.

She offered him his Corona, and he took the beer and set it on the nightstand. Turning back to her, he slid his palm down her leg, cupping the flesh of her calf and then pushing the delicate sandals off her feet. Then he slipped his hand under the skirt of her sundress, caressing the firm flesh of her thighs. She shivered, her eyes drifting closed. Her legs parted and he slid his hand closer to her center.

He teased her through the silk of her panties, feeling it dampen in response to his touch. He slid one finger under the elastic leg band of her underwear and traced her opening. Her legs thrashed.

Her breathing was rapid now, her breasts straining the buttons on the bodice of her dress. He leaned down and tongued her nipple through the fabric. She gasped his name and held his head to her.

"Open your dress, *chère.*"

She fumbled with the buttons and he watched her. Finally she had them all undone down to her belly button. The fabric shielded her from his gaze except for a thin strip of creamy flesh visible through the opening. The rounded curves of her breasts moved with each breath she took.

"Bare yourself to me," he said, his voice a growl.

She nodded and pulled the bodice open. Her nipples were starting to harden, the pale pink flesh becoming darker. He pushed her skirt to her waist and looked down at her, spread before him like a sensual feast. God, he was hungry for her.

He kissed her abdomen and then moved lower, to the very heart of her. When her hips lifted in response, he parted her and thrust his tongue into her body. She tasted exquisite and he felt himself hardening almost painfully. The need for her was too demanding to resist. She moaned his name.

He kissed his way up her body, scraping his teeth over her until he found her mouth, all the while thrusting his fingers deep inside her. He sucked her into his mouth and pulled, needing to quench the thirst he had for Jayne. She was gasping his name now, her nails biting into his shoulders.

He felt her tightening around him and then she screamed as her body convulsed. He lifted his head and looked down at the woman in his arms. She met his gaze with a totally unguarded expression, and he felt sucker-punched by the emotion he saw shining in her eyes. He was unworthy of her love. He wasn't the guy she needed to make her dreams come true.

Adam stepped back and stripped off his shorts, then pulled her panties down her legs and tossed them aside without saying a word. She bit her lower lip and watched him, the emotions on her face joined by something else. Fear, pity, anger? He wasn't sure, but he sensed she knew he was running.

He didn't want to think or feel anything other than the hot desire pulsing through his veins. This was the one thing he could count on.

He took a pillow from the head of the bed and pushed it under her hips. Knowing this was the best that he could give her, he brought her to a second climax with his mouth on her.

Shuddering, she reached for him, taking his erection in her hand and pulling him toward her body. "I need you."

He needed her, too. He needed her to promise she'd never leave him, but he knew he couldn't ask for that. And he sensed her keen eyes saw that desire inside him. He flipped her over on her back.

Adam used his teeth to pull her dress down her body and drop it on the floor. He held his hand at the small of her back when she would've turned over.

He traced her spine with his tongue, then dropped nibbling kisses there, caressing the rounded curves of her hips and tracing the seam between her cheeks with his tongue. He parted her legs and slid up over her body, rubbing himself against her until she raised her hips.

Adam lifted her slightly and slid into her body from behind. Clasping her hands in his, he moved slowly, though he clamored for release. His penis was so hard he felt as if it had been years since he'd found satisfaction instead of the few hours since they'd left their suite this morning.

But he wanted this to be more than just release. He wanted to give Jayne more than she'd ever experienced with any other man, so he kept his thrusts slow and steady. He bit her neck at the base and tickled the flesh there with his tongue.

And when he knew he couldn't hold back any longer, he slid his hands down her sides and held her hips while he thrust harder and harder into her. He felt her body clenching around his a second before release surged through him and he emptied himself into her.

He collapsed on top of her, shutting his eyes so that he wouldn't have to see what Jayne was feeling. But as he lay there in a euphoric haze, he prayed that she'd agree to live with him, for the glimpse of heaven he'd just had in her arms was the closest thing to paradise he'd ever found.

Eleven

Jayne spent the afternoon of her second to last day on the island with Didi in the spa, being pampered. Adam had given her the time off and said he didn't want to see her until she relaxed. Jayne couldn't believe the changes that their time here had wrought in him. He was a different man than she'd known before, and he'd put to rest her girlish dreams of Mr. Right. Adam was so much more compelling.

Still, much of their relationship was up in the air. She didn't know what he planned to do when they returned. Jayne had already drafted a resignation letter in her head and knew that she'd gambled her heart for Adam. But she felt confident she was going to come up a winner.

Though he was careful to never make promises he couldn't keep, she knew that Adam didn't want to let her go. He'd told her as much last night in bed, in the quiet hour just before dawn when life seemed almost perfect.

"I can't believe we're leaving here in a few days," Jayne said to Didi now. "You must love living here. It's like heaven on earth."

"Not really," the older woman replied with a small smile. "But I do like it."

"Why are you selling it?" she asked. Didi and Ray weren't really old enough to retire, and they seemed to enjoy the resort. Ray was always in the beachfront bar, telling stories and entertaining the guests.

"Ray and I have to travel a lot with our jobs. So staying here isn't an option anymore."

Jayne wondered about the couple. They kept their lives private, but Jayne had been studying couples since the second grade, when one of the girls at her school had asked if Jonathon O'Neil, her mother's current lover, was Jayne's stepfather. She hadn't realized until that moment that other families didn't have a rotating male in their households.

"What is your job? I hope you aren't offended if I say so, but neither of you seems to know a lot about the hotel industry."

"We don't. We're more experts on human nature. That's why finding a couple in love to buy the resort is so important."

"I can see how that would be nice, but from a business standpoint it lacks a little credibility."

"Are you always business-minded, Jayne?" she asked.

Jayne tried to be, because life had proved easier that way. But lately she seemed to be more family-minded. Her head filled with images of her and Adam and a brood of kids that belonged to them. Of she and Adam creating the family they'd both always craved and never had. Of them living in a big house and growing old together.

She sighed. "Usually. Lately, though, not as much."

"It seems to me humans use business to occupy their lonely lives instead of seeking out comfort in each other."

"Perhaps. But there is a very nice feeling that comes with success."

"Yes, there is."

A timer went off at the drying station, letting them both know the nail polish on their toes was dry. Jayne slid her feet into the spa thongs she'd brought, and stood. "I'm glad we got to spend the day together."

"Me, too. I'll see you at dinner," Didi said, exiting the spa.

Jayne took her time gathering her bag and walking up the path toward their suite. She would miss the island. Even if Adam purchased it she probably wouldn't be coming back here for a while. She thought about her travel goals and decided she'd add in all the countries she wanted to visit, not confining herself to the fifty states. She could get used to island living.

When she reached the suite, she opened the door and found Adam on the phone. She observed him as he talked, making notes on the pad in front of him. His wore a pair of shorts and a Hawaiian print shirt that he'd left unbuttoned.

She dropped her bag inside the doorway. Adam looked up and smiled at her, gesturing that he'd only be a few more minutes. She took a bottle of seltzer water from the minibar and settled on the love seat, watching him. She didn't listen to his conversation, just let the sound of his voice wash over her.

Closing her eyes, she tried not to put too much hope into thoughts of the future, but knew it was too late. She'd fallen hard for Adam.

"How was the spa?" he asked, dropping down on the cushion next to her.

He put his arm around her shoulders and hugged her close to his side, then bent down and kissed her. He'd told her a couple of times how her mouth enticed him.

"Relaxing. I enjoyed it. Thanks for insisting I go," she said, when he lifted his head.

"No problem. I know I can be demanding sometimes, but I wanted you to see that I can also be generous."

Adam was acting a little odd. She couldn't put her

finger on it, but something was different about him. "I already knew that."

"That's right, you're the—what did you call it?—facilitator of my generosity?"

"That's right. You're usually very generous toward women at the end of your affairs. Should I be worried?"

"No. This isn't like any relationship I've had before."

Me, either, she thought. He opened his arms and she sank against him. Sometimes she felt so vulnerable around him that she thought she'd break into a million pieces. But when he held her she felt safe and that her love was a good thing. She closed her eyes now and breathed deeply of his spicy masculine scent.

"I have another present for you."

"Where?"

"On the bed."

"You don't have to keep buying me things."

"I like to spoil you, Jayne."

"Why?"

"Do I need a reason?"

"No," she said, but it worried her. She knew Adam well enough to realize he used his money as a shield.

"I want tonight to be special for you, and my present is just part of that."

He ushered her into the bedroom, where she found an exquisite cocktail gown lying on the coverlet.

Adam left her to dress, saying he had plans to make. Her heart beat faster as she realized he must have something important on his mind if he was going to all this trouble just for her.

"Buona notte," Ray said in a greeting when they arrived in the lounge for a predinner drink. Adam would be happy to have the resort business out of the way so he could concentrate on Jayne. He no longer felt a burning need to destroy this place and make it into something it wasn't. He could appreciate the charm of the resort and separate that from the betrayal he'd felt with his father.

"I've made arrangements for us to dine on our private veranda," their host announced. "The sunsets are spectacular there."

"Thanks, Ray."

"Nothing but the best for our ladies tonight."

Didi rolled her eyes, but a smile lingered on her lips, and for the first time since Adam had met the couple, they seemed to be almost at peace with one another.

"Our ladies should always have their heart's desire."

"Jayne said you'd found the treasure box?" Didi asked as Ray led the way through the public rooms to their private quarters.

"We did. The trail isn't that hard to find. Even if you decide not to sell to me I think you should jazz it up a bit. Jayne spoke to a professional treasure hunter and he'll help embellish the tale and make the search a little harder.''

''Good suggestion, *compare*. I've implemented many of things you recommended. You really know your stuff when it comes to resorts.''

Getting the resort didn't matter as much as it once had. Adam was happy to have had this time on the island with Jayne. If they didn't acquire Perla Negra, he'd buy some land and develop his own resort based on a legend. Maybe he'd bring Jayne with him to oversee the construction. ''It's what I do. And frankly, I love it.''

Ray nodded. He took a cigar out of his pocket, but Didi reached over and snatched it out of his hand before he could light it. ''I've always felt the same about my job. Sometimes this one gives me *agita*. But otherwise things aren't so bad.''

''I can tell. Not many owners would hold out for the kind of buyer they want for their resort. I can tell the property means more to you than just a quick buck.''

''Well, you can't take it with you,'' Ray said with a laugh. Didi joined him.

They arrived at a large veranda, where a table was set for four. An ice bucket stood next to the table with a magnum of champagne in it.

''We got off track,'' their hostess murmured. ''Did you like the cave? Did you read the incantation?''

"I did. I took a stone," Jayne said quietly.

"I'm not surprised. What about you, Adam?" Didi asked.

"I did, too."

Jayne glanced at him from under her eyelashes, and he felt her reproval. When Didi excused herself to check on the dinner, and Ray followed her inside, Jayne turned to Adam. "You don't have to lie to them about it. They know you're too...practical to believe in that legend," she stated.

He said nothing, just reached into his pants' pocket and pulled out the stone to show her. She swallowed hard and stared at him. Adam felt that strange feeling in his chest again when she gazed up at him, this time with her heart in her eyes.

He caressed her face, tilting her head back and capturing her lips with his own. Sipping carefully at her mouth, he treated her like the rare treasure she was. He found it hard to believe that feisty, sassy Jayne was the answer to the empty part of his life.

"What did you wish for?" she asked after a minute.

"I'm not supposed to tell."

"I hope it comes true, Adam," she said fiercely.

"You're the only one who can make that happen."

She trembled under his hands. "Same here, stud muffin."

"Woman, you are asking for it."

"When have I ever pretended not to be?" she said.

"Let's have a toast," Ray said, stepping back outside before Adam could respond.

But Adam reached down and pinched Jayne's backside surreptitiously as they walked to the table. She gave him a look over her shoulder that made his blood flow heavier and his body stir to life.

Didi joined them a moment later, carrying a tray of hors d'oeuvres. Setting it on the table, she took a flute from Ray. Once they all had a glass in their hand, Ray slipped his arm around Didi and looked at Adam, raising his flute. "To the new owner of La Perla Negra. May he find love and happiness as well as prosperous times ahead."

Adam felt a queer sensation in his stomach as he realized what Ray was saying. He couldn't lift his glass and drink, but turned to Jayne and took her in his arms. She stretched up and gave him a kiss that shook him. His hands were trembling with desire when she sank back onto her own chair.

"Now we drink," Ray said.

"Now we drink," Adam agreed. They all sipped the Asti and Adam took it as a sign. They sat down at the table. Everything in his life was coming together. After years of working and struggling to right the wrongs of the past, he was going to have the resort that had led his father to ruin. Adam had a woman by his side who he knew was a partner in business as well as in life. And he was finally coming to terms with the fact that his heart wasn't as well-guarded as he'd always believed.

Dinner went by in a haze of pleasure, and Adam realized that the only thing missing from his life was a commitment from Jayne. But in a few hours, he'd have all the pieces in place.

Jayne emerged from the bathroom wearing her one-of-a-kind negligee.

"Close your eyes," Adam told her.

She did as he asked. Beneath her feet she felt something soft and cool, and peeking from under her lashes, she saw rose petals. Their fragrance filled the room.

"I can't keep my eyes shut for long," she warned, crossing the room toward the sound of his voice. She hated not being able to see. It made her feel exposed.

"Sure you can, *chère*. It's worth it, I promise," he said. This time his voice came from a different direction.

She turned toward it, sliding one foot at a time in front of her to make sure she didn't run into anything. "I can't stand it. I want to see."

Large and warm, his hands covered her eyes. "I had no idea you were so impatient."

"It's not really impatience as much as vulnerability. I hate that feeling."

She felt his lips brush hers, with a back and forth motion that made her stand on her toes and try to pull him closer. But when she reached for him, he wasn't where she'd expected him to be.

"You don't have to seduce me. I'm already yours," she said, knowing the words were true. There was no other man who could make her forget the painful lesson she'd learned as a child, and remember her secret dreams. No other man who tempted her to believe that those dreams might have a chance of coming true. No other man who made her forget a time when they hadn't been together.

"Are you?" he asked. He touched her face, tenderly tracing her cheekbone and the line of her nose. She wished she could see his expression. Adam gave so little away and she was tired of trying to guess at the depth of his feelings.

"You must know that I am," she said. She wasn't going to hide from him.

They were scheduled to go home tomorrow afternoon, and she knew that once they returned to New Orleans, reality would come crashing down. She'd prayed that reality might mean a marriage of her life with Adam on the island and the one they'd had before. But she couldn't tell what he felt. She thought he loved her...well, knew he cared deeply for her. The way he held her at night, so close and tight, told her it had to be more than sex.

"Good," he said, quiet satisfaction in his words.

He wrapped a length of silk around her head, covering her eyes. "How's that?"

"Adam…"

"What?" His mouth was against the back of her neck, moving slowly downward. "You can't see and my hands are free."

She swallowed her doubts and said, "Do your worst, stud muffin."

He chuckled and then wrapped her in a tight embrace. "I intend to. But first…"

He lifted her in his arms and carried her somewhere. She felt the warm sea breeze a minute before he set her in one of the rattan chairs on the balcony. She loved his strength and the fact that he was a toucher. She'd never been petted like this by any man, but Adam was always reaching for her.

"Wait here a minute. I have to take care of a few last-minute details."

She heard him leave, and leaned her head against the back of the chair, tilting her face up to feel the breeze more fully on her skin. The roar of the surf was a pleasant accompaniment to the wind rustling through the palm trees and bushes.

"Miss me?" Adam asked a moment later, speaking directly into her ear.

Before she could answer, he tugged her to her feet and removed the blindfold. She blinked a few times and realized that all around her candles flickered. Not just on the balcony, in wall sconces and tiki lamps that had been mounted to the railing, but also behind her, in the bedroom.

"Are we celebrating Perla Negra?"

"No, *chère.* I'm celebrating you."

Oh, God. Her heart started beating so fast she thought it might burst from her chest. She'd hoped and prayed that he might come to care for her, but she'd never expected a gesture this big. This grand. But she should have, because Adam wasn't a man given to subtlety.

"Jayne, I have something important to ask you."

"Yes?" She could scarcely breathe as he turned toward her. Her heart raced, and for a moment she was afraid to believe the dreams she'd harbored for so long were at long last coming true.

"Will you live with me?"

She shook her head, unsure she'd heard him correctly. Adam gave her the gentlest smile she'd ever seen grace his face.

"*Chère,* we're great partners in the office. I think blending our personal and professional lives is…the perfect solution."

Jayne was still trying to understand what he'd said. But she didn't doubt his sincerity. Adam was offering her the one thing he'd never offered any other woman. And she wanted to accept. But her own dreams were hard to let go of. "I'd like nothing better," she said.

"Great. I knew you'd see it my way."

Sadly, she realized she hadn't been clear. This conversation wasn't something she'd anticipated. She wished she'd had time to make a plan of action for it. "I'm sorry, Adam. I didn't mean that the way it came out. If we're going to live and work together, why not get married?"

"Marriage is the one risk I won't take."

"Being your mistress is the one risk I won't take."

"Dammit, woman, I'm not asking you to be just a mistress."

Her heart ached for him. And she almost changed her mind and agreed to be his, whatever the terms. But in the end she knew they'd both end up hating each other. Adam watched her and she shook her head at him.

"Dammit, you think this is easy for me? You know how I feel about office romances and yet I'm willing to do this for you."

"Don't make this about me. What you're offering is designed to give you everything *you* want."

He took her in his arms. "Don't say it like that. This is the best I can do right now."

Tipping her chin back, he stared into her eyes. "Please, *chère,* give this a chance. I'm not ruling out marriage forever but I need more time."

She stared up at him, cupping his jaw in her hands and, standing on tiptoe, kissed him with all the love she had in her body. "I don't need more time, Adam. I already know I love you."

"And I care deeply for you. I know our relationship can be a successful one."

"Being your mistress or live-in lover will kill me, Adam. I've spent my entire life, built my entire self-image around not being like my mother. And I have to be honest here—I want kids." She didn't need a marriage certificate to stay with the man she loved if he was committed to her. She could tell by the look in his eyes that he didn't want them. But she held her breath for his answer.

"No."

Her heart broke then and she realized that she'd fallen in love not with Adam, but with the man Adam could be if he'd ever let go of the past and start to dream of the future.

She shook her head and pulled out of his arms, backing away from the man that had seemed like her future.

"Oh, *chère*."

She went to the dresser to find her clothing. Pulling them on carefully, praying she could finish dressing and get out of there before she started crying. She refused to let Adam's last image of her be one with tears running down her face.

"So this is it?" he asked.

"Yes. You'll have my notice on your desk Monday morning."

"I thought you loved me," he said, quietly.

She stared at the man she knew. The man who'd carefully crafted a life of loneliness because he believed that was the only safe way of living. She wanted to reach for him. But didn't.

"I do. But that doesn't mean I don't value myself."

"What's that supposed to mean?" he asked. He grabbed his pants from the floor and shoved his legs into them.

"Nothing. I was being nasty." And she had been. In fact, she'd hurt herself with the words. She knew that Adam felt more for her than the other women he'd seen. And if she were a different kind of person—one who didn't need order and structure—she might be able to accept the offer he'd made, and hope that some day he'd come around.

He crossed the room, but when he reached for her, she took a step back. She didn't want him to touch her now. She felt as if she might break into a million pieces with very little provocation.

"Please, don't go. I'll give you anything you want if you stay."

"Anything?" she asked, knowing he wasn't offering his love and that she'd never ask for it.

"Yes. Name it—a new car, a fur, jewelry. *Anything.*"

She knew then that despite the fact that she'd laid her soul bare to him, Adam had never seen the real her. Or he'd know that the trappings of a mistress were the last things that would make her stay with him.

"There's nothing you have that I want," she said.

And this time she meant it. She had wanted his love, but knew that he didn't have enough in his cold soul to give her.

"You don't mean that."

"I do. You've surrounded yourself with material objects and status symbols. I need more than that to be happy. Actually, I need a lot less than what you have. What I want doesn't cost anything."

"No, you just want my soul," he said.

Until that moment she hadn't realized that she'd asked him for his soul. But she did want it. After all, he already owned hers. "I thought it was an even trade."

"Well, it's not. I'm not like you, Jayne. I don't look at the world through rosy glasses. I've lived in the real world my entire life and I know what you're looking for is a fairy tale."

She stalked to the door. She wasn't talking to him anymore. "I'm not giving you two weeks."

"I'm not giving you a reference."

"I don't need one from you."

She took her purse and ran out, slamming the door behind her. She didn't look back, but let the tears run unchecked down her cheeks.

Twelve

Adam punched the wall nearest him and cursed savagely. How had things gotten so out of control? His hand throbbed, and as he surveyed the room he realized that he couldn't stay here another minute. Every time he saw those candles and the rose petals he was reminded that his seduction had gone terribly wrong.

Why had the setup that had worked in the past failed him? Probably because Jayne wasn't like every other woman who'd been in his life. She was so damn stubborn.

He knew what she wanted. In fact, if the burning in his gut was any indication, he already loved her. But he wasn't saying the words out loud.

And he wasn't marrying her. He couldn't. He'd tried to make her understand that if she just waited a little longer, gave him time to adjust to having her in his life, he might be able to. But that wasn't good enough for Jayne.

He sank into the armchair, gazing around the hotel suite, which was like so many others. But in the last ten days, Jayne had made this feel like home. She'd given him someone to share not just the business of his life with, but also the other things. The part that no one had ever been interested in before. Jayne actually cared that he loved being on the water, and had arranged for them to go sailing every afternoon, even though she was still afraid of the ocean.

But did that mean she would stay with him? Did that mean that once he married her she wouldn't get bored and move on? And did that mean that he'd always want her in his life?

His fear was not that Jayne would leave him, he acknowledged. His real fear was that someday he'd leave her. And he couldn't stomach the thought of hurting her that way.

Hell, he needed a drink. He grabbed a shirt from his closet and shoved his feet into a pair of loafers, heading out the door and straight for the bar.

His hand still throbbed, but he felt as if he deserved the pain. God knew it was less painful than the feelings deep in his gut, feelings that he refused to acknowledge came from Jayne's leaving.

He ordered a glass of single malt and sat down at one of the deserted tables in the back of the smoky lounge. The band had long since finished their last set and the place was almost empty.

"Eh, *compare,* still celebrating?" Ray sat down across from him.

The waiter brought his drink, and Adam downed half the glass. "Bring me another."

"Where's Jayne?" Ray asked.

"I have no idea," he stated. He could guess, though, and the images in his head made him want to get drunk so that he couldn't see them anymore. He didn't want to picture Jayne as he'd last seen her—face pale, tears glistening in her eyes. She'd run from him, and he cursed himself for making her go.

"Women problems?" Ray asked.

Adam sneered at the older man. "Not me. I'm the expert when it comes to relationships."

Ray leaned back in his chair and reached in his pocket for a cigar. He lit it and then glanced around the room. "Don't get me wrong, pal, but what kind of expert is sitting in a bar an hour before closing time, drinking alone?"

"Not much of one," Adam said, downing the rest of his drink. He knew nothing when it came to women or relationships, which was probably why he'd lost the one woman he wanted to keep.

"Want to talk about it?" Ray asked, exhaling a thin veil of smoke.

"You really get into that father confessor thing?" Adam said with derision.

"Nah. It's just that I've been there."

"With Didi?" Adam asked. It would make him feel better to know that he wasn't alone.

"No, not with her. I let someone else slip away because I didn't realize that the love of the right woman can make a man stronger. You know, a better man."

"Well, Jayne doesn't see that. She can only see…" Adam didn't know what Jayne saw when she looked at him. He suspected it was some romanticized version of him. But he'd bet his business that she didn't any longer.

"What can she see?"

"That I'm not the kind of guy to give her what she wants in order to be happy," Adam said at last. He toyed with his highball glass, rolling it in his palms.

"Oh, hell."

"Listen, if you no longer want to sell me the resort, I'll understand. You should know that I was setting you up from the beginning. Jayne was my assistant, not my mistress," Adam said.

"But that changed."

"Not for long," he answered.

"This has nothing to do with the resort. Listen, you go after Jayne and talk to her."

Adam wished it were that simple. But he wasn't

willing to lay his soul on the line for her. And she'd settle for nothing less. "She won't listen to me."

"You have to try," Ray insisted.

"You're taking this father confessor thing too seriously. It's over between Jayne and me. The only thing left to do is move on."

"*Madon'*, why the hell did I think this would be easy?" Ray said, stubbing his cigar out in the ashtray.

"What are you talking about?" Adam asked. What in blazes was he thinking, discussing this with a man who was nothing more to him than a business acquaintance?

"Look, *compare,* I'm not really a resort owner. I'm a matchmaker sent from heaven to make sure that you and Jayne fall in love."

"Well, you screwed up," Adam said, not believing what Ray said for a minute.

"You're telling me! But you're not leaving me any options here. If you won't talk to her..."

Ray might be a little bit insane, Adam decided, flinching when the older man took his hand. Then, suddenly, the walls around them were spinning, and when they finally stopped he and Ray were outside a bar in New Orleans.

"This isn't real."

"Keep telling yourself that, *compare,*" Ray said.

"Why are we here?"

"I don't know. This is the place you brought us to."

Adam recognized the bar. He hadn't been in there since the night of his divorce, when he'd gotten rip-roaring drunk. "Take me back to Perla Negra."

"Not yet. Let's go inside."

Ray nudged him toward the door and Adam went in. He scanned the dimly lit interior and had no trouble finding himself seated at the bar. He looked so damn young and scared.

"Another round?" the bartender asked.

"Keep 'em coming," the younger Adam said. He downed the glass of cheap whiskey. In those days he hadn't been able to afford the good stuff.

"Here you go," the bartender said.

"Thanks, man."

When the bartender turned away, Adam stood and announced to the room in general, "From this moment on, I will not be a victim to women and their emotional traps."

Glasses were raised in support, and the younger Adam sat back down and finished his drink.

The older Adam stared in shock. He'd built his life around a vow he'd made when he was twenty-one and not sure of himself, he realized at last. He knew what had happened the next day: he'd made a solid business plan and used the impetus of Susan leaving him to start Powell International. He'd worked hard for six months before he met Rhonda, his first mistress. He'd still been too raw to really want more than sex from a woman.

So they'd come up with an arrangement that had worked for both of them. And what had been a temporary stopgap in his relationships had become the norm.

In an instant, Adam found himself back at his table in the lounge at Perla Negra. Ray was nowhere to be seen, and Adam wondered if he hadn't dreamed the entire episode. He rubbed his forehead. The liquor had given him a buzz. And something Jayne said kept echoing in his head.

Just because I love you doesn't mean I don't value myself.

Adam realized that he hadn't been valuing either of them, but letting the past keep him in the dark.

He left the bar, hoping it wasn't too late to find Jayne. The only chance either of them had for happiness was together, he was certain. He loved her, and not saying the words out loud didn't keep him safe, it kept him out of the sunlight that was Jayne.

Jayne had asked the bellman to call her a cab. Waiting outside the resort, she refused to cry. She was angry at Adam and at herself. How could she have misjudged him?

But had she? She'd spent her entire life hiding from the men who scared her. She'd been engaged to Ben because he was safe and didn't make her heart beat faster. Only now, looking back, did she acknowledge that his leaving her didn't hurt as badly as this moment with Adam.

Was a ring really that big of a deal in the big scheme of things? Her heart said no. But having a family was. And not just for herself. Adam needed it, too. He needed to have his own children so he could shower them with that unconditional love that she knew was buried deep inside him.

Was she a coward for leaving like this?

"Jayne, thank God, I caught you."

"I'm not going to change my mind," she said softly.

Adam glowered at her and she felt the force of his determination. "Yes, you will. I'm going to convince you."

"With another practiced seduction?" she asked sarcastically. She still ached from their last encounter, and she wasn't sure she was up for another one.

He shoved his hands in his hair, looking almost frantic. Her heart beat a little faster as she realized that he'd come after her. Adam had never gone after any of his women before. He just moved on.

"No. That was a mistake."

Her cab pulled up in the driveway and the driver got out. "You called for a taxi?"

"Yes. I'm going to the airport."

"No, she's not," Adam stated.

"Yes I am."

"Listen, it's late, and I don't want to sit here while you two fight it out," the cabbie said.

Adam took some money from his pocket, shoved it at the cab driver and said, "You're free to go."

As the man got back in his car and drove away, Jayne glared at Adam. She hated that he thought he could use his money to arrange life to suit him.

"Come with me," he said to her.

"Not now. When you get home, come to my place and we can talk."

"Forget that," he said. Reaching out, he lifted her over his shoulder, then snagged her bag in one hand.

"Put me down!"

"No."

She struggled and he smacked her butt with the flat of his hand. "Stay still, dammit."

He stalked through the nearly empty lobby. Jayne stopped struggling and instead fought the urge to wrap her arms around his waist. She didn't want to leave, and it seemed he didn't want her to go.

He set her on her feet once they were in their room. She stared up at him, not recognizing this man. There was something in Adam's eyes she'd never seen before. Something that looked like…love.

He took her face in both of his hands and lowered his head, whispering something against her lips. Tracing them with the tip of his tongue, he deepened the kiss when she opened her mouth. She sighed, lifting her hands to his chest.

She didn't want to live the rest of her life without Adam. Tears started falling, and Adam brushed them away with tender fingertips.

"Don't cry, *chère*. Don't cry."

He rocked her in his arms, and she knew that she'd stay no matter what he offered this time. And that hurt her deep inside, because she'd always believed that someday she'd meet a man who'd want her for herself and want all of her.

"I love you."

She stared up at him, sure she hadn't heard him correctly. "I don't need the words."

"Really? I think you do. And I know you deserve them."

"Adam, I've only been gone thirty minutes. How can you love me?"

"I saw the light, and it was a scary experience. I'll tell you about it later. I think I've loved you all along, Jayne."

"I want to believe you," she said.

"But you don't. Hell, don't leave me again, *chère*. If you go, I'll become the hard shell of a man that you think I am now.

"I need you, Jayne. You make me a better man and I think I make you a better woman. You shouldn't have run away from me."

"I couldn't stay. I was afraid."

"Well, you don't have to be anymore. No more hiding for you, Jayne."

"Do you mean it? Because if you changed your mind—"

"I was afraid of that, too. But I can't change my mind. Woman, you own me heart and soul."

She swallowed against the tears burning the back of her eyes. This time they were tears of joy, for she knew that Adam didn't say things he didn't mean. If Adam committed himself to her, he'd stay with her.

And there was no mistaking the love shining from his eyes.

"I love you," she said at last.

"I love you, too. And I always will."

He lifted her in his arms and carried her into the bedroom. He settled her in the center of the big bed and then reached into the nightstand drawer for something.

It was a long, narrow jeweler's box. "I ordered this for you. It's not traditional, but then, neither are we."

He piled the pillows against the headboard and sat back against them, then pulled her onto his lap. He held her loosely in his embrace while he removed the sapphire tennis bracelet from the black velvet case. He fastened the clasp around her wrist.

"We're getting married," he said.

"You're not asking me?"

"Do I really need to?"

"Yes," she said. She wanted to have a really good story to tell her grandkids one day. Though it'd be hard to top him carrying her through the lobby over his shoulder.

"Will you marry me?"

She wriggled her eyebrows at him. "Only if I can call you stud muffin."

He groaned. "Okay."

Her heart felt incredibly light and she turned on his lap, wrapping her arms around him. "I can't wait to be your wife."

He took control of their embrace and they didn't talk for a long time as clothing was hastily discarded and they sealed their vows of love and commitment with their bodies.

Afterward Adam curled himself around her and held her fiercely in his embrace. They talked of the future and of their dreams for their life together. Jayne realized that Perla Negra had worked its magic and she'd found her heart's desire.

Epilogue

I looked out over the ocean. All my life I'd lived near it, but never really seen it. I'd only thought that the beach was a good place for a smuggling drop and that water was a dangerous place to dump a body because sooner or later it washed up on shore.

But today, with the sun setting on the horizon and the minister saying words of love and lifetime commitment, I realized there's a lot of beauty on earth. Too bad I didn't learn that lesson while I was still alive.

Adam gave a Jayne a kiss that was too intense for public viewing. I turned away and felt Didi's hand slip through my arm. I'd never admit it, but I'd enjoyed her company on earth.

And once she'd stopped dressing like my maiden aunt, she looked great.

"Nice job," she said softly.

I took her hand in mine and started walking down the beach. "I know."

"Pasquale, you need to work on humility."

"Babe, I never really grasped why pretending you don't know you're good at something was a good thing."

"I thought I warned you about calling me babe."

"You might have," I said.

She chuckled. "You've got too much charm for your own good."

"Ah, babe, I didn't think you'd noticed."

"Save it for your couples," she said. And I felt my body start to dissolve. She might think she'd had the last word this time, but she'd gone soft against my side before she disappeared. Maybe it was the fact that I spent so much time around couples falling in love, but I was starting to like Didi.

* * * * *

Silhouette

Desire

From reader favorite

Sara Orwig

STANDING OUTSIDE
THE FIRE

(Silhouette Desire #1594)

All his life, Boone Devlin has been a
high-flying no-commitment bachelor who
drew women like flies to honey, but never
stayed with any one for very long. So what
happens when he falls head over heels for
the one woman who seems entirely able
to resist his charms?

Seems like this time the boot is
on the other foot....

STALLION PASS:

TEXAS KNIGHTS

Where the only cure for
those hot and sultry
Lone Star days are
some sexy-as-all-get-out
Texas Knights!

Available July 2004 at your favorite retail outlet.

BABY AT *HIS* CONVENIENCE

by
Kathie DeNosky

(Silhouette Desire #1595)

Katie Andrews wants a strong, sexy
man to father her child. When former
marine sergeant major Jeremiah Gunn
walks into her café, Katie believes she's
found the perfect candidate. Trouble is,
Jeremiah has some conditions of his
own before he'll agree to give Katie
what she wants—including turning sweet,
shy Katie into the type of brazenly
uninhibited woman he's used to.

Available July 2004
at your favorite retail outlet.

If you enjoyed what you just read,
then we've got an offer you can't resist!

Take 2 bestselling love stories FREE!

Plus get a FREE surprise gift!

Clip this page and mail it to Silhouette Reader Service™

IN U.S.A.	**IN CANADA**
3010 Walden Ave.	P.O. Box 609
P.O. Box 1867	Fort Erie, Ontario
Buffalo, N.Y. 14240-1867	L2A 5X3

YES! Please send me 2 free Silhouette Desire® novels and my free surprise gift. After receiving them, if I don't wish to receive anymore, I can return the shipping statement marked cancel. If I don't cancel, I will receive 6 brand-new novels every month, before they're available in stores! In the U.S.A., bill me at the bargain price of $3.57 plus 25¢ shipping and handling per book and applicable sales tax, if any*. In Canada, bill me at the bargain price of $4.24 plus 25¢ shipping and handling per book and applicable taxes**. That's the complete price and a savings of at least 10% off the cover prices—what a great deal! I understand that accepting the 2 free books and gift places me under no obligation ever to buy any books. I can always return a shipment and cancel at any time. Even if I never buy another book from Silhouette, the 2 free books and gift are mine to keep forever.

225 SDN DNUP
326 SDN DNUQ

Name	(PLEASE PRINT)	
Address	Apt.#	
City	State/Prov.	Zip/Postal Code

* Terms and prices subject to change without notice. Sales tax applicable in N.Y.
** Canadian residents will be charged applicable provincial taxes and GST.
  All orders subject to approval. Offer limited to one per household and not valid to current Silhouette Desire® subscribers.
  ® are registered trademarks of Harlequin Books S.A., used under license.

DES02   ©1998 Harlequin Enterprises Limited

COMING NEXT MONTH

#1591 COWBOY CRESCENDO—Cathleen Galitz
Dynasties: The Danforths
Newly hired nanny Heather Burroughs quickly won over Toby Danforth's
young son with her warmth and humor, but Toby's affection was harder to
tap into. This sexy cowboy was still reeling from his disastrous divorce and
wasn't looking to involve himself in any type of relationship. Could Heather
lasso this lone rancher into settling down?

#1592 BEST-KEPT LIES—Lisa Jackson
The McCaffertys
Green-eyed P.I. Kurt Striker was hired to protect Randi McCafferty and
her baby against a mysterious attacker. After being run off the road by this
veiled villain, Randi had the strength to survive any curve life threw her.
But did she have the power to steer clear of her irresistibly rugged
protector?

#1593 MISS PRUITT'S PRIVATE LIFE—Barbara McCauley
Secrets!
Brother to the groom Evan Carter was immediately attracted to friend of the
bride and well-known television personality Marcy Pruitt. While helping to
pull the wedding together, they found themselves falling into a scandalous
affair. But when Miss Pruitt's private life became public knowledge, would
their shared passion result in a wedding of their own?

#1594 STANDING OUTSIDE THE FIRE—Sara Orwig
Stallion Pass: Texas Knights
Former Special Forces colonel and sexy charmer Boone Devlin clashed
with Erin Frye over the ranch she managed and he had recently inherited.
The head-to-head confrontation soon turned into head-over-heels passion.
This playboy made it clear that nothing could tame him—but could an
unexpected pregnancy change that?

#1595 BABY AT *HIS* CONVENIENCE—Kathie DeNosky
She wanted a strong, sexy man to father her child—and waitress
Katie Andrews had decided that Jeremiah Gunn fit the bill exactly.
Trouble was, Jeremiah had some terms of his own before he'd agree
to give Katie what she wanted…and that meant becoming his mistress.…

#1596 BEYOND CONTROL—Bronwyn Jameson
Free-spirited Kree O'Sullivan had never met a sexier man than financier
Sebastian Sinclair. Even his all-business, take-charge attitude intrigued
her. Just once she wanted Seb to go wild—for her. But when the sizzling
attraction between them began to loosen *her* restraints, she knew passion
would soon spiral out of control…for both of them.

SDCNM0604